To Louise and Jim

Eben Kruge

HOW *A CHRISTMAS CAROL* CAME TO BE WRITTEN

Merry Christmas!

[illegible signature]

December 4, 2012

Eben Kruge

HOW *A CHRISTMAS CAROL*
CAME TO BE WRITTEN

Richard Barlow Adams

Eben Kruge
How "A Christmas Carol" Came to be Written

Cover Art Work Design by Erick Martin

Frontispiece Art Work Design by Andy Lemoine

Library of Congress Control Number:		2012920413
ISBN:	Hardcover	978-1-4797-4232-5
	Softcover	978-1-4797-4231-8
	Ebook	978-1-4797-4233-2

This book was printed in the United States of America.

To order additional copies of this book, contact:
Xlibris Corporation
1-888-795-4274
www.Xlibris.com
Orders@Xlibris.com
125203

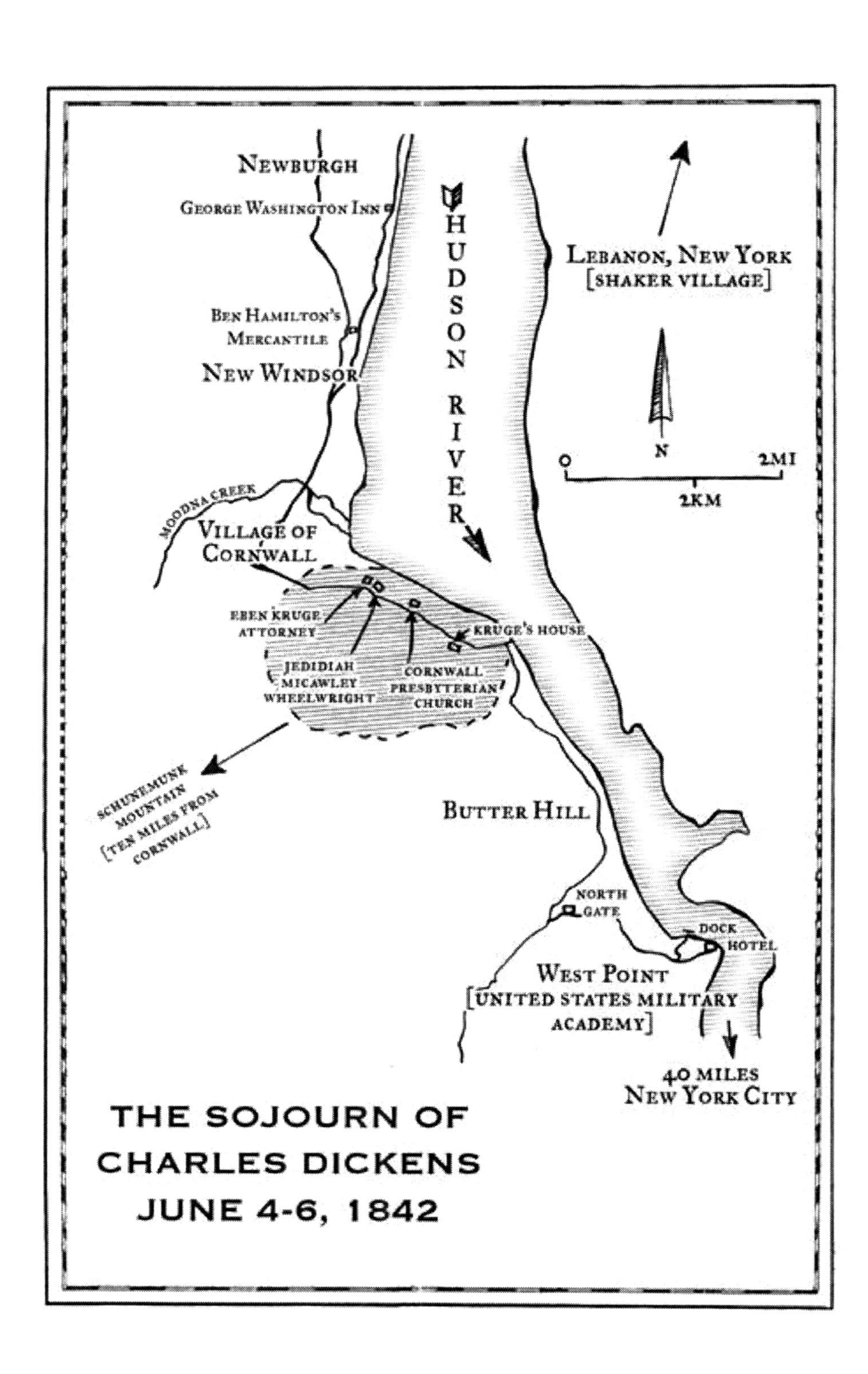

Newburgh
George Washington Inn
Hudson River
Lebanon, New York
[shaker village]
Ben Hamilton's
Mercantile
New Windsor
N
0
2MI
2KM
Moodna Creek
Village of
Cornwall
Eben Kruge
Attorney
Kruge's House
Jedidiah
Micawley
Wheelwright
Cornwall
Presbyterian
Church
Schunemunk
Mountain
[ten miles from
cornwall]
Butter Hill
North
Gate
Dock
Hotel
West Point
[United States Military
Academy]
40 miles
New York City
THE SOJOURN OF
CHARLES DICKENS
JUNE 4-6, 1842

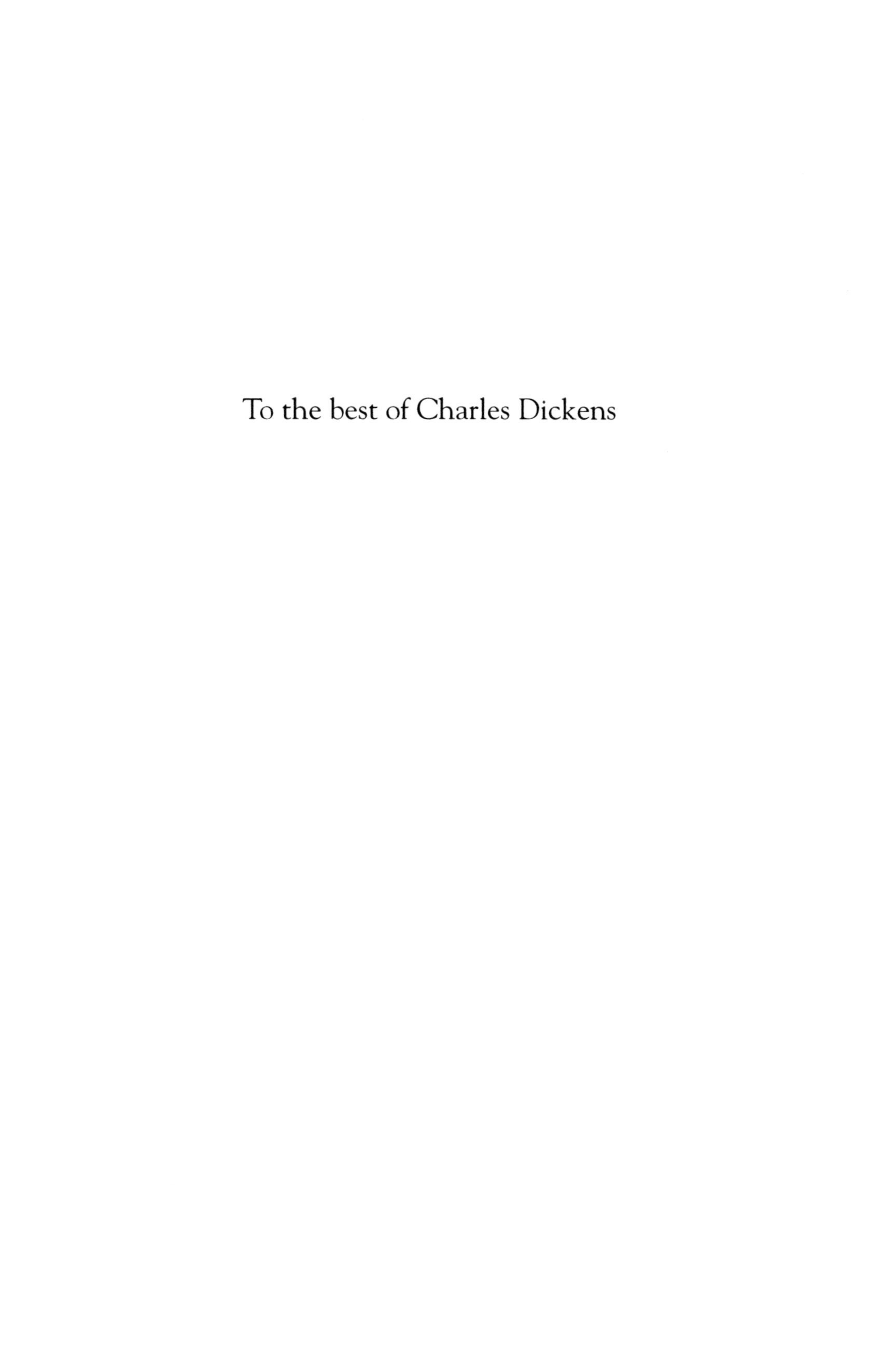

To the best of Charles Dickens

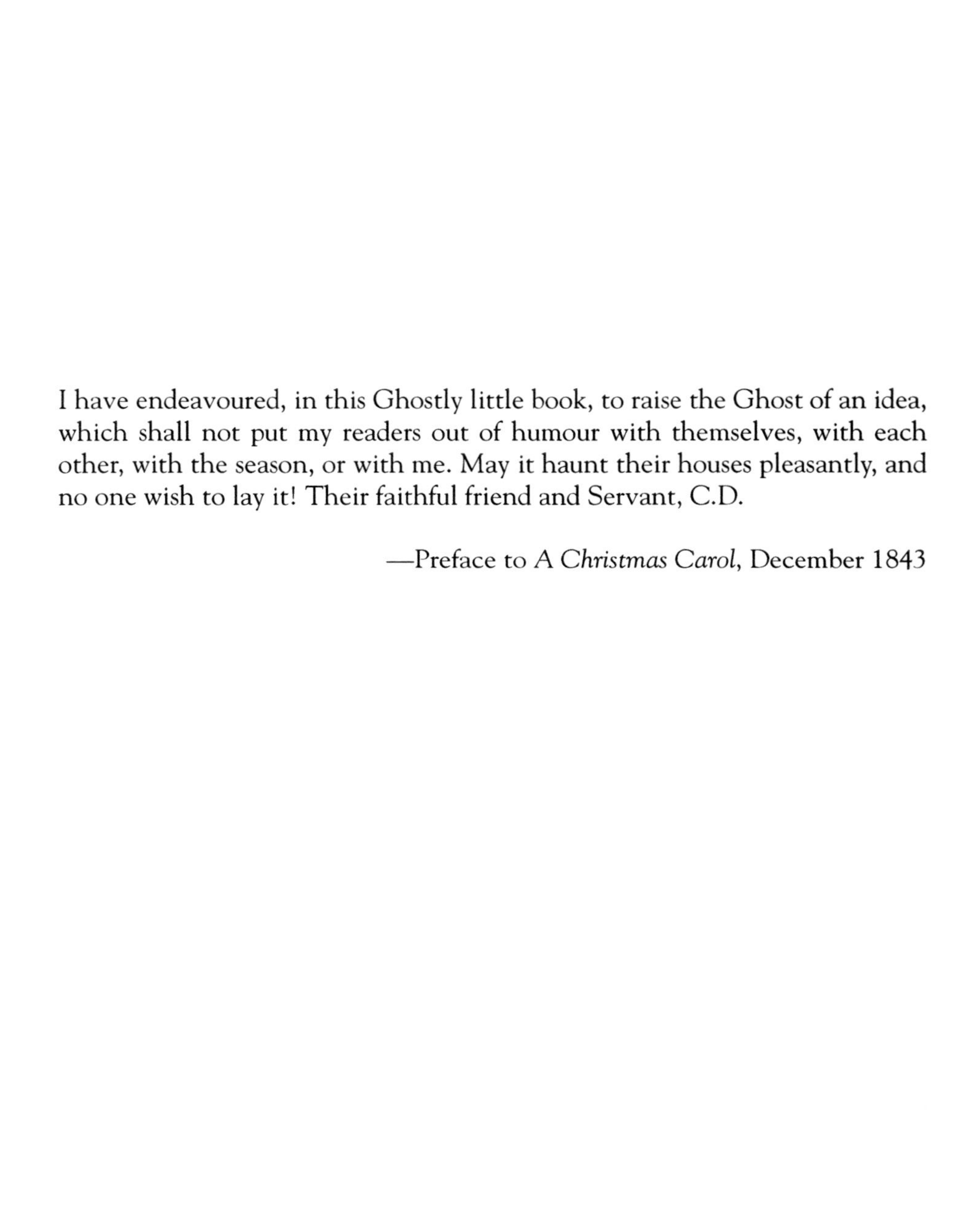

I have endeavoured, in this Ghostly little book, to raise the Ghost of an idea, which shall not put my readers out of humour with themselves, with each other, with the season, or with me. May it haunt their houses pleasantly, and no one wish to lay it! Their faithful friend and Servant, C.D.

—Preface to A *Christmas Carol*, December 1843

Introduction

What is it about Charles Dickens's *A Christmas Carol* that propels so many of us, annually, to reread the "ghost story of Christmas" and watch its many film and play productions? What is the fascination? Did we not "get it" the first time, or fifth time, or twentieth time? Or is it, simply, that we are yearly drawn to old friends with whom we've "grown up," and who have witnessed our "growing up," friends like Jacob Marley, Bob Cratchit, Tiny Tim, old Fezziwig, the ghosts of Christmas past, present, and future, and, of course, Ebenezer Scrooge. And are we not drawn to the wonderful themes in the story that weave in and around the real meaning of Christmas?

And what of the man who penned the *Carol?* What was he like—the writer, social reformer, businessman, husband, father, son, sibling, and friend? What circumstances framed his past and present when he sat down to write the *Carol?*

Eben Kruge is a story that explores these and other questions behind why Charles Dickens wrote *A Christmas Carol* in 1843, the first of five short fictions in a six-year period, termed his Christmas stories, which would include *The Chimes* (1844), *The Cricket on the Hearth* (1845), *The Battle of Life* (1846), and *The Haunted Man and the Ghost's Bargain* (1848). *Eben Kruge* is a story that invites us into the life of Charles Dickens.

The author

Preface

Is it entirely unreasonable to believe that the story that follows could have actually happened? That, of course, you must decide. But not the reality of what transpired thereafter, the form of which is documented history, and which for human kind, at Christmas time, has warmed hearts, brightened spirits, inspired goodness, and drawn people to their better nature perennially ever since. And so you should know, this and more being true, that . . .

On January 3, 1842, Charles Dickens, age twenty-nine, already England's foremost writer and social activist, set forth with his wife Catherine for North America on the steam-packet, Britannia. Over the next five months, chronicling his observations and opinions, he visited nearly two dozen cities as far south as Richmond, as far west as St. Louis, and as far north as Quebec. During his travels he is hosted and feted almost nightly, including an invitation from his dear friend, Washington Irving, to visit the American writer's Sunnyside home in Tarrytown, New York. In early June, his trip nearly over, Dickens and Catherine travel up the Hudson River from New York City to the village of Lebanon, where they spend the night. The next morning, they visit a nearby "Shaker Village," Dickens intent on witnessing the religious sect's exuberant dancing, an experience that is denied him by the sect's elders. Thoroughly frustrated and earlier than planned, he and Catherine retrace their steps to the Hudson and gain late passage south as they enter upon the story that follows . . .

Chapter One

The 55-foot paddlewheel steamer, Glenwood, battled five-foot waves whipped up by a storm that had in the past half hour materialized from nothing. The sky was an inky swirl of gray and black. In the torrential rain, the boat entered the giant S-turn of the river that gave the point of land called West Point its name. Stern of the boat, a bolt of lightening illumined the morose sky, and a cannonade reverberated up and down the river. Catherine Dickens, her lower lip quivering, was hard against the lower deck rail, bent over, her mouth agape. "Oh, God. Dear God, no more, please . . ."

"You must come inside, Catherine!" Charles Dickens shouted against the roar of river and engine, holding onto the railing with one hand and Catherine with the other.

"What . . . so I can be sick on the others?"

The shrill blast of a steam whistle sounded above them, and Dickens trained his eye on the bow and beyond it on the ethereal shoreline bearing shadowy figures. Suddenly gears in the engine room began to grind and screech in a way Dickens thought might tear them apart. But the boat's paddlewheel finally stopped and grudgingly reversed, and he braced for impact against the dock, surprised by barely a thump.

"Lock her down, lads." A voice commanded from above. "West Point. The United States Military Academy. All ashore, going ashore," declared another.

Dickens felt a hand upon his shoulder. A crewman cocked his head toward Catherine. "Sir, I expect the sooner you get the missus ashore the better."

"Oh, yes . . . thank you, God!" Her mouth covered with a handkerchief, Catherine buried her face in her husband's shoulder as he followed the crewman.

Dickens led Catherine down the gangplank and past two longshoremen. On the dock, he was surprised to find they were the only ones to disembark. As the boat pulled away, the dock was soon empty, the longshoremen having disappeared into the mist.

"They are expecting us, aren't they Charles?" Catherine asked, shivering.

"The captain assured me that we would be met once the boat made its stop."

A full ten minutes later, a mule-drawn omnibus with the words *West Point Hotel* across its side appeared out of the fog. Its uniformed driver descended from a high perch. "Sir, I've come as quickly as I could. We . . . we were not expecting you."

"I understand, and I thank you for coming as quickly as you have."

The driver opened the coach door, and seeing Catherine's pallor, turned to Dickens. "The woman, she is all right?"

"She's fine."

Unconvinced, the driver nodded. "I'll attend to the luggage, sir."

Dickens helped Catherine inside, and once inside took her hand. "Look at me, Catherine."

Catherine presented a face drained of color, her eyes glazed.

"Better?"

"Just take me home, Charles. I want to be buried in England."

"Nonsense. You have an impressionable stomach. That's all." He put his arm around her. "I too want back in England, to kneel upon its earth, to thank God for its being. I'm ready to forgive its sin and history. England I understand. England is predictable. This United States is too vast, too infantile, too much a spineless conundrum; at the same time everything and nothing, promising what it cannot deliver, delivering what it promised not to, deserving whatever fate lay in its path."

"I fear I have set you off, Charles," Catherine said.

"Nonsense. A night here, two in the city, and then to home."

Catherine covered her mouth again. "Oh, God . . . another boat!"

Dickens checked his watch, surprised to find that it was only half past six. When the omnibus crested the bluff to a vast open plain, he observed a tall pole bearing the flag of the new nation. The flag bore thirteen stripes and twenty-six stars, and beside the flagpole was a small cannon, which he took to be the reveille gun. Various other artillery pieces, large and small, were displayed along the crest road. The rain had stopped and the dark clouds had begun to peal back, revealing lighter shades of gray. A few minutes later, the omnibus ambled up a cinder-paved lane to a large, stucco-finished, three-story structure.

The driver dismounted his perch, opened the door, and extended his hand.

Dickens helped Catherine up the steps, across the veranda, and into the hotel. At the registration desk, a middle-aged man greeted them. "Dear me;

looks like you got the whole of it. Had we only known, sir. Anyway, we need you in some dry clothes, don't we? How many nights, sir?"

"Just tonight."

"Excellent. If you will sign here, please." The clerk spun the registration book around and handed Dickens a quill. After Dickens signed the book, the clerk spun it back around. "And a very warm welcome to you . . . Mr. and Mrs. Charles Dickens." The clerk hesitated, his eyes widening. "Boz?"

Dickens nodded, with a disingenuous smile.

"Well now, that is quite something, isn't it?" The clerk tapped his chin. "With the board of visitors here for examinations and so many families in for graduating cadets, we are a bit pinched for rooms, but I'm sure we can do something." The man leafed through his reservations. "Ah, yes, since you are here but for a night, I can give you room 14, a fine room indeed, with a grand view of the river." He slid a key across the desk and gestured to the second floor. "On your right, third door on the left. And, please, trust your luggage to me."

Dickens drummed his fingers on the counter. "Thank you, and supper?"

The clerk pointed down the hall. "Eight o'clock, sir, until ten. Just through the double doors." The man grinned from ear to ear and muttered under his breath, "Old Boz himself."

Catherine suddenly covered her mouth, suppressing a groan.

The clerk instinctively closed the register. "Is the lady all right, sir?"

Dickens held up a hand. "She's fine."

Upstairs, and after their luggage had been delivered, Dickens drew back the curtains in the hotel room and raised the window, exclaiming, "My dearest, you must see this. The clouds are nearly gone. The sun is . . ."

"Charles," Catherine groaned, already spread eagle on the bed with eyes closed. "Please, close the curtains. I need rest. Everything is still moving. Just let me sleep."

"Not until you are out of those wet things." He coaxed her to her feet and helped her undress and into a nightgown. After changing his own clothes, he kissed her on the forehead. "I'm going to look about."

To Dickens's relief, the registration desk was unattended, and once outside on the wide veranda he quickly digested his surroundings. The color of everything was crisp in the fading sunlight that followed the storm. To the north and east was the broad dark river, called by some the North River, which, with the Erie Canal and Champlain Canal, was the principal thoroughfare to America's Great Lakes and Canada. The river was flanked on either side by the verdant Highland hills that Washington Irving declared enchanted, and adding to the enchantment was a brilliant rainbow. To the west and south, beyond an expansive plain, the constructions of the forty-year-old United States Military Academy trumpeted regimen and discipline.

"Mr. Dickens, sir?"

Dickens turned to find a tall, stout, full-bearded man dressed in something akin to a naval uniform. Dickens judged the man to be in his fifties.

"Mr. Dickens, I am Captain William Roe, the hotel proprietor. I wanted to personally welcome you . . . to assure you that you will have your privacy." Roe extended his hand.

Dickens's countenance improved instantly, and he took Roe's hand. "For that, sir, I am much obliged."

"Of course." Roe followed Dickens's gaze across the plain.

"Most quiet here," Dickens observed.

"All this week and next, the cadets have their year-end examinations, and a sad time for those that don't make the mark."

"A truly beautiful piece of ground, your West Point, cupped between river and rock . . . most striking."

Roe nodded. "Indeed, we are much secluded."

Dickens reached for his pipe, filled the bowl, and lit it. After a few puffs, he turned to the Captain. "You wouldn't by chance have some cigars?"

Roe smiled. "Follow me."

Inside, Roe produced from behind the registration desk a tray of assorted tobacco products.

Dickens nodded approvingly and, after sniffing twice as many, selected half a dozen cigars. "Please, put these on my account."

"Certainly, sir." The Captain did a mental tally and jotted a number on a small ledger. "I understand from Robert that your wife is not well. I am very sorry to hear it. If there is anything I can do, you must let me know."

"You are too kind. And as to my wife, it is my fault. I push her too hard, and she doesn't complain. I should have let her stay in city. The pitching on the river . . . her stomach . . ."

"Yes, the afternoon storms can blow up quickly." Roe rapped a knuckle on the veranda railing, and gave Dickens an affecting smile. "If there is nothing else, Mr. Dickens, I will leave you to your thoughts."

"Actually, there is one thing more, sir. I should very much like to purchase a few fingers of brandy or your American whiskey, your bourbon. That and a cigar will do much for my spirits."

Roe gave Dickens a look. "Sir, this is a military post . . . with the cadets and all . . . I am sorry, but ours is a temperate establishment. I am not to sell any form of alcohol. To do so would cost me my position."

Dickens was incredulous. “Good God, man! You mean to tell me no one on this post takes a drink? Is this not the United States? And will the frustrations of my day have no end?”

Roe offered a sympathetic smile. “Mr. Dickens . . . while I am unable to sell you what you’ve requested, should you choose to forfeit your privacy, I would be more than honored to have you and your wife join me for a private supper in my quarters. There you may name your drink, and we’ll enjoy a fine wine. After all . . . I am a Navy man.”

Dickens clasped Roe’s hand, warmly. “Hang the privacy, Captain, I need a drink, and I am most grateful for your offer, though I cannot yet speak for my wife.”

“Excellent. It being near seven now, why don’t we say seven-thirty or eight. I’m just at the end of the hall, room 2. Do you enjoy a good steak?”

Dickens smiled. “Your American beef is the best, and, if it is all the same to you, I am inclined to seven-thirty.”

Chapter Two

Dickens returned to his hotel room, removed his shoes, and slipped into bed. He rested recumbent against the bed board beside Catherine. She rolled over towards him, her eyes closed. He stroked her hair, and perceived in her face a measure of color.

Catherine opened one eye.

Dickens leaned over and kissed her on the cheek. "How are we doing?"

"I don't know . . . maybe a little better."

"You are my brave girl, aren't you?"

"Not so," she mumbled. "I am an albatross."

"My dear, you are not. And soon enough you will be with the children."

Catherine groaned. "Don't make me cry. That I left our little ones is more than I can bear."

"Cheer up, mother. In three weeks, we'll be a family again."

Catherine stretched and yawned, and gathered herself up next him, drawing his hand to her breast. "I fear this trip has claimed too much of me . . . my nerves have gone all directions. I could sleep a week."

"Sweet Catherine," Dickens said, assuringly. "Your constitution is not a mean one, but like everything has its bounds." He kissed her again. "You must know how grateful I am for your companionship these five long months in this vast, big country. Had you stayed in England, I might have gone raving mad for the houndings and distractions we've endured. I am a writer, for God sakes, not a royal. These Americans have worn me out with their attentions and expectations. My hand aches with the shaking of it in every ballroom, assembly hall, restaurant, coach, boat, and train. Oh, for a quiet evening with dear Forster and Macready, to bond with them again, to drink and make merry as only the three of us can."

His comment made Catherine smile. John Forster and William Macready were his best friends and closest confidants, Forster a godparent of one of the four children, Macready the namesake of a second child, and all the children in the excellent care of Mr. and Mrs. Macready. "And I miss our parties,"

Catherine said. "Ours are the best, Charles, and you—you are the most famous host a party ever had."

"We do enjoy a good time, don't we," Dickens said with a wink.

"Charles?" Catherine's tone was more serious.

"Yes, love?"

"You will soften it, won't you? Your readers need not know all of your thoughts about their new country."

"My *American Notes?*" Dickens said, referring to the title he had selected for his observational account.

Catherine nodded.

"I cannot lie, and neither can I ignore what claims voice. The defense these people give to slavery is unconscionable . . . a blatant disregard for their own Constitution. And so many of the people are self-centered to a degree they are best taken in small doses." Dickens gave Catherine a wry smile. "But neither will I sacrifice my readership to rhetoric that exceeds its purpose. There are many fine qualities about the country and its public institutions, and there are many hundreds of wonderful people we've met who would acquit themselves famously in any society. No . . . I will temper my pen."

Catherine returned a weak smile. "Good. We need to give these sweet people time to grow up. That is what sister Mary would have said."

At her words, Dickens's countenance took a turn.

Catherine drew him close. "I'm sorry, Charles. That was unkind of me. It's just that . . . she's been gone such a long time, I thought . . ." Mary Hogarth, her younger sister, had for a short time been part of the Dickens household, and much help to Catherine when she birthed and nursed their first child, Charley, and later when she became pregnant a second time. That at age seventeen, Mary had become violently ill in the space of an evening and died before morning was more than the two of them could bear, and that she had died in his arms was for him sorrow beyond sorrow.

His eyes moist, Dickens forced a smile. "Exactly what our Mary would have said."

Catherine squeezed his hand. "She was the sweetest of sisters and the dearest of souls, and, Charles, you so honored her. When you penned little Nell's death in *The Old Curiosity Shop*, it broke hearts across nation, around the world. And every tear shed for little Nell was shed for our dear, dear Mary."

Dickens patted her leg and made a brave face. "But we've had some incredible times in this wicked land, haven't we? And by the time we get back to England, we'll have forgotten the worst and every frustration." He manufactured a smile. "Interesting how that works."

Catherine squeezed his hand. "You are the most resilient man I know, and these Americans love you."

"Still," Dickens added, "I did expect better of a people with so many freedoms."

"Charles," Catherine's tone was admonishing.

"Right." Dickens said with a wink. "I should allow God to do the rest."

Catherine glanced out the window at the hued sky. "Such a pity that you and Washington weren't able to bond again. You two are soul mates. In his presence, you ignore me greatly."

Dickens nodded. While in New York City early in the trip, he had received the older Irving daily for three straight weeks, and to one breakfast, Irving had brought the venerable William Cullen Bryant.

Dickens smiled. "Though, in truth, my dear, I feel he is with us . . . in this, his land of Rip Van Winkle and Sleepy Hollow." Dickens made a wild face. "Hear me, my precious, the unnatural abounds in these hills."

Catherine found herself laughing against her will to suffer.

"We've an invitation, dear," Dickens said, softly. "Captain Roe, who runs the hotel, has invited us to dine with him in his quarters. We are to have American beef."

Catherine winced at the thought of eating, or even leaving the bed. "Why don't you two have a man's evening? I will get a head start on my seven days of sleep."

"Are you sure? The Captain is most engaging. I suspect he could make you laugh."

Catherine shook her head. "Charles John Huffam Dickens, Boz to your readers, I do love you, my man of faith." And with that, she slid under the covers.

Chapter Three

Dickens knocked on the door to the Captain's room at precisely seven-thirty, and was greeted with a smile and an inquiry about Catherine. Dickens explained that Catherine's only desire was to sleep, and that the notion of a meal was wholly disagreeable, but that after dinner he might take her some hot tea, a biscuit, and a piece of fruit. Roe said he would arrange for it, and then explained that his home and family were in Newburgh, up river, but that during the busier times of the year he lodged in the hotel. The Captain's room was no larger than Dickens's, but boasted a second armoire in which Roe kept extra clothes, personal effects, some books, and a stock of liquors and wine, all under lock and key. A table was set beneath the open window, and through the window Dickens saw upon the river a few white sails and a steam packet. The table was arranged for three with white bone china, polished silver, and crystal, and Roe reset the table for two. A bottle of red wine sat uncorked on the center of the table next to a small vase with a seasonal flower arrangement. From a decanter, Roe poured a golden liquid into two glasses, handing one to Dickens.

"Your health, sir, and a quick recovery for your wife." The Captain made a slight bow.

Dickens clinked the Captain's glass. "And your health and your most thoughtful and gracious hospitality." Dickens rolled the liquid about on his tongue, feeling its burn as it passed down his throat. He smiled. "Your American whiskey?"

Roe nodded. "From Kentucky."

"And now my favorite." Dickens swirled the bourbon in his glass, gazed out the window, and mused, "Washington Irving did not overstate the beauty of this place."

The Captain laughed, "Actually, Washington overstates everything, but then, that is his nature."

"A friend?"

"For many years."

"Perhaps a bit prone to overstatement, but your finest and most read pen," Dickens declared in his friend's defense. "With a brilliant mind."

Roe grinned. "And vivid imagination."

Dickens sipped his whiskey. "Exactly. And possessing social gifts I wish I had."

Roe placed his glass on the table. "Which is why he is now our minister to Spain."

"And how is it you know the man?" Dickens inquired.

Roe reflected. "First, I suppose, as runny-nosed grammar school kids on Manhattan Island, our fathers both merchants. But even then he showed imagination. And of course we grew up and in different directions, but have stayed in touch. Before he bought Sunnyside, he was often my guest here. A very consistent soul."

Dickens gazed out the window. "Before coming to America, Washington and I corresponded for most of two years, the two of us separately waging war against international copyright infringement, and coming to know each other through our letters. It was his idea that I make the American tour, and that I approach my publisher for funding, which I did." He turned to Roe. "And which will allow me to write about your country."

Roe nodded.

"When Washington and I finally met face to face, we had already read much of what the other had written, and had much in common. Catherine and I thoroughly enjoyed his Sunnyside home, and he was the consummate host. It was there, I learned of his appointment to Spain." Dickens smiled. "And you are right, he has a most vivid imagination . . . I am sorry not to see him again before we leave."

"Which is when, sir?"

Dickens told him.

"I'm curious," Roe said. "What do you think of us? We, Americans?"

Dickens expected the question. It was universally asked. And he was usually given to a polite, commending reply. But measuring Roe, he sat back in his chair. "Sir, I think you have some disgusting habits, like spitting tobacco whenever and wherever you please. I had the singular displeasure of attending a session of your congress in your capital city. The floors of both your senate and house of representatives were a battleground of spittle, with the least affected areas being those around the spittoons." Dickens broke off with a smile. "I suppose I should apologize."

Roe returned the smile.

A suited man from the hotel dinning staff served dinner. The beefsteak, on the rare side, trimmed with roasted potatoes and asparagus, was much to Dickens's liking, as was the full-bodied Bordeaux. Over dinner, Roe continued to question Dickens about his travels and observations, and Dickens continued to answer honestly. When the table was cleared, Roe produced a decanter of brandy and two cigars, and when they had fired their cigars, Roe excused himself, soon returning with six books, and placing them on the table.

Dickens grinned.

"Let me see if I can order these chronologically." Roe arranged the books; books entitled *Sketches of Boz, The Pickwick Papers, Nicholas Nickleby, Oliver Twist, The Old Curiosity Shop,* and *Barnaby Rudge.*

Dickens nodded. "You have, and you honor me with the effort."

"These reside in our pitifully small library in a corner of our parlor. As you can see, they are nearly worn out with reading, except for *Barnaby Rudge,* which we only just received. I thought, perhaps . . . you might be so kind as to sign them," Roe said, expectantly.

Dickens reached for *The Old Curiosity Shop,* opened the book to the copyright page, and with a pained expression shook his head. "Sir, to do so would be an offense to me."

"An offense?"

"Captain Roe, my publisher is Chapman and Hall." He pointed to an entry on the copyright page. "I have no idea who these brigands are, and have received no royalties from their sales."

Roe examined the copyright page. "Ah, I see. And I'm sorry to know it. Yet, for my part, I do not know, otherwise, how we would have your books."

"Which is my problem, not yours. Regardless, you've made the excellent point that many of your fine countrymen have made—you like my work. And for that, I am most grateful. You would think I could be less critical of you people."

"Pshaw. Our skin is thick enough, or should be."

"Should be . . ." Dickens mused. "And of that I will learn soon enough." Dickens took a sip of brandy. "Now, if I may ask you a question . . . Tell me, sir, what is it you like least about my writing?"

The question caught Roe by surprise.

"Be candid," Dickens said. "I appreciate the fact that you enjoy my stories, but answer me honestly. What least appeals to you about my work? Criticism is the best teacher, and no less for me."

Roe considered, and then picked his words carefully. "What I like least? Yes, well, I suppose you could shorten some of your sentences, certainly some of your paragraphs. At times they seem endless . . . when my eye falters, I have to go back and start all over . . ."

Dickens smiled.

"Indentions are a wonderful thing, sir. A single indention on a page in one of your books is a thing to be cherished . . ."

Dickens laughed good-naturedly. "Fair enough, and now, what is it you like best?"

It was Roe's turn to laugh. "Why, I suppose everything else—your characters, your scenes, your dialogue, and your spiderous plots. Your characters are more real than most people I know. Take *The Pickwick Papers*, your Pickwick and company—how such characters can be imaginary is beyond me. Which leads me to ask . . . ," Roe hesitated.

"Yes . . ." Dickens pressed.

"You have only just met me, and know scarce little about me, but, say, you were to plant me in your next story, in any fashion of your choosing, what, pray tell, might that look like?"

Dickens laughed heartily. "You, sir, who have saved my life, at least for the night . . . well, let me think on it." Which Dickens did, and after he had, he rose to his feet and looked down upon the mariner.

"Upon arrival at Yorkpudding," Dickens began, a smile forming on Roe's face, "the carriage was met by the proprietor of the Yorkpudding Inn, a Captain Roswell, who's former service in the king's navy was marked by his attire and distinctive carriage, dressed as he was in naval colors, polished boots, and tri-cornered hat, his comportment exuding a comfortable mix of dominion and humility. Evidence of duty, honor, and love for country and queen was borne on his face, a black leather patch covering his right eye."

Roe laughed aloud.

"The Captain," Dickens continued, "greeted individually, and with singular approbation, those in the carriage; receiving first the most honorable Mr. Samuel Pickwick, founder of the Pickwick Club, and in succession, Messrs. Augustus Snodgrass, Nathaniel Winkle, Tracy Tupman, and Mr. Pickwick's personal valet, Sam Weller."

Roe exclaimed, "Oh, to have been part of the Pickwick Club."

"Had we only met earlier," Dickens said, suggestively.

"So, how is it you do it, sir?" Roe asked, shaking his head. "How is it you come up with so many characters, all different and unforgettable, each bearing his own past and present?" Roe ran his finger across the books arrayed on the table. "How do you populate your stories with such vivid beings and not repeat yourself? Now, there is your gift, Mr. Dickens!"

"Yes, well, in that, sir," Dickens said, presenting a glum face, "you have touched a tender nerve. For what is in my stories, comes from here." Dickens tapped his temple. "You see, my characters certainly most of them, are as real as you and me. They are flesh and blood people I have come to know personally or through intermediaries. And I must confess the cupboard," Dickens tapped his temple again, "is nearly bare. I would give an eyetooth for a truly distinctive spirit to enliven a story."

Roe nodded, as Dickens sipped his brandy.

"I don't know that it is my place," Roe said, offhandedly.

Dickens leaned forward. "Do you know of such a person, Captain?"

"Perhaps . . ."

"Someone with a unique story?"

Roe refilled Dickens's glass, and then his own. After taking a few sips, he gave Dickens an equivocal look.

Dickens again leaned forward. "Yes?"

"There is a man, I'm told, and just recently, whose black turned to white quite literally overnight. Not that I know the man or the details, and have only met him once, and that an unpleasant meeting. Strangest thing I've ever heard, but Ben Hamilton, a friend visiting from New Windsor, swore it's so."

"And the man's name?" Dickens asked.

"Eben Kruge. But he is not here. He lives and offices in Cornwall."

"Which is where?"

"Maybe five-miles north, along the river."

"So . . . an hour buggy ride?"

"Perhaps more. But you are leaving tomorrow . . . I don't see . . ."

"Will he take visitors?" Dickens interrupted, the rejection by the Shakers fresh in his mind.

"He is an attorney . . . he will take a client."

"Of course he will." Dickens said, laughing. "And the last boat to the city is the one that dropped us off?"

"That's right."

"Then there is time, Captain Roe," Dickens declared cheerfully, rising to his feet. "That is, if I may have use of a hotel buggy . . . first thing in the morning?"

Roe nodded. "Of course."

"And, my wife . . . might I burden you to look after her? She should awake in better spirits. Perhaps a tour of the Academy. She would like that."

"Again, of course," Roe said.

"Bravo! Bravo my dear man! I will be down at first light, which should put me in Cornwall by eightish. If Kruge is a man of business, I should catch him in by then. Say, four or five hours with him, and I should be done, and, say, another hour and half back to the hotel . . . that should work just fine. Perhaps you could assist Catherine with the luggage, getting it to the dock." Dickens was beside himself with the prospect and with the man, Eben Kruge.

"But sir, in truth, you know nothing about Kruge, and he may be away from his office. Surely you want to know more before embarking on such a venture?"

"And spoil all the fun?"

Chapter Four

At five o'clock, Dickens awoke to the crack of the reveille gun, scarcely a hundred yards from the hotel. As the flag of the new country was raised, Dickens raised himself. The evening before, as Catherine managed a cup of tea and half a biscuit, he had made known his intentions, and she had expressed no little joy at the prospect of being able to do anything or nothing the next day.

Downstairs by five-thirty in a pair of black trousers, braces, and a white shirt and carrying his suit coat, cravat, black felt top hat, and a leather folder with writing materials and four cigars, he eschewed a full breakfast that would have delayed him a full hour. Instead, he accepted a gingham-lined wicker basket of hard rolls, a wedge of cow cheese, and two corked bottles of beer. He found Captain Roe and a liveryman in front of the hotel readying a highly polished black-lacquered one-horse buggy.

"And a very good morning to you, Mr. Dickens," Roe said, offering a slight bow.

"As early as I've been up the entire trip," Dickens declared. "And I miss it. Many's the time I've walked twenty miles the streets of London in the dead of night."

"For your characters?"

"And their worlds."

"That cannot have been without danger," Roe said, handing Dickens a sketch map. "The directions, you see, are quite simple. And there is a bag of oats in the drop for the horse. We call him Colonel. But don't feed him until you reach Cornwall, and he's watered."

Dickens nodded, a boyish grin on his face. "Then, I'll be at it, sir." He shook Roe's hand and mounted the carriage seat, and after settling himself, tagged the horse's rump with the buggy whip, and hollered, "Colonel, take me to Cornwall!"

Ten minutes later, Dickens was at the Academy's North Gate, halted by a guard he thought too young for a uniform. Dickens explained himself, that he would be returning in the afternoon and hoped he might be allowed back on post. His attempt at humor was lost on the young man, who only nodded and raised the gate bar. A furlong beyond the gate, Dickens came to an intersection and a sign with an arrow pointing right, to Cornwall. The road proved generous and well maintained, the ruts having been recently filled in. In quick succession, Dickens passed two large wagons loaded with cordwood. Both drivers greeted him, the second warning of a coyote.

Since the sun had yet to crest the hills east of the river, the light was soft, and the landscape shadowless. As was his habit, Dickens registered the line and nature of everything. The smell of earth and forest, seasoned with morning dew, was a delight to his nose. The air was still, and all about him were trees and shrubs in more variety than he could name. Accenting the greens and browns were flowers of every color and form. Colonel's hooves beat a pleasant rhythm upon the earth and stone, and Dickens felt an exhilaration he hadn't felt in months. Beyond his common senses, a sixth sense was at work—that of imagination—as it always was in London in the dark of night.

As the road snaked the shoreline two hundred feet above the river through a canopy of elms, maples, and oaks, he reflected upon a wife dearly loved, and who loved him, more so than he could return, whose only fault was wanting more of him than he could give. He thought of Charley, Mamie, Katie, and Walter—four impish children, ages five, four, three, and one, whose cherub faces brightened his morning and nightly prayers. He thought of home on Devonshire Terrace, a house exceeding any he might have imagined as a child. And he thought of his passion to write and the gift to do so, and how at the age of twenty-five he was the talk of the Commonwealth, and now, the world, envied by those he had once envied.

A rustling sound on the hillside put Colonel to a trot. Dickens looked back, but saw only a doe, her head down in the tall grass. Pulling on the reins, he whispered, "Easy, boy. Nobody's going to get you."

As Colonel clopped along, Dickens reflected on the myriad events that ran together since their arrival in America, himself the honoree in gatherings of tens, hundreds, and thousands, sitting with an American president, meeting and conversing with the likes of Henry Wadsworth Longfellow, now a cherished friend, Oliver Wendell Holmes, Harriett Beecher Stowe, Edgar Allen Poe, Daniel Webster, and Henry Clay. And invading the pleasantness of his thoughts came another, a recurrent admonition, that he *never stop writing, not ever; all else depends on words, even breath.*

As the forest light increased, so did the weight of obligation, chief among them his *American Notes*. What would be its purpose, its premise? What was needful? Less than a month into the visit, he had regretted the assignment, that if faithfully done, could not end well. Such thinking gave way to other musings—commitments, deadlines, and finances. And from this he fell into a moodiness, which until recently had never darkened his thoughts, that perhaps life lived thus far was enough, that an early death might be a blessing, and that those who would grieve him would soon enough survive; that living too long, to wrinkle and fail in ways others had, whose lives seemed not to end and who had strayed from their better path, was not a good thing.

The buggy came upon a stretch where the bows of the trees on either side knitted together to form a hollow, the road shaded to a dusky darkness. And with it, the temperature fell a dozen degrees. Dickens thought of taking on his coat. At the haunting of an owl, Colonel pulled hard against the reins, Dickens supposing that the animal sensed what he sensed. Still, he whispered comfort to the horse, counseling that no phantom, no dark rider was in pursuit, that such things were nonsense.

The hollow behind them, clear openings to the broad river and distant verdant hills and a rising sun behind them increased Dickens's anticipation. Around a sharp bend in the road, an expanded shoulder presented an unobstructed view, and Dickens pulled back on the reigns. Colonel anticipated perfectly, and stopped at the edge of the bluff. Dickens delighted in the panorama, and popped the cork on one of the bottles of beer. He took a long draft. With his pocketknife, he cut thin slices from the cheese wedge, and breakfasted on the cheese and one of the hard rolls.

As he ate, gazing at the river, he considered how poorly matched the Thames was against it. Thus, and otherwise invested, he was unaware of the approach of a wizened old man with a wooden staff, who, despite his age and being on foot and carrying a burlap bag over his shoulder, moved at a surprising pace.

"Good morning, sir," the old man announced himself sharply, a form of lisp in his speech.

Dickens turned. "And a hello to you, fine fellow. I was just enjoying your river." Dickens wondered at the kerchief across the man's face, as there was neither dust upon the road nor wind to blow it. Dickens cocked his head rearward. "Going to West Point?"

"I am," the old man said. "I take you as English."

"And you would be correct," Dickens replied, "and soon must leave your beautiful country."

"Beautiful, yes, but in the summers, leastwise here, scorching hot every day. A body must move early or late, or wilt to the bone."

"You are coming from Cornwall?"

"The road goes only there, and then on to Newburgh. But, yes, born and raised in Cornwall."

Dickens noticed the man eyeing his hard roll. "Have you breakfasted, sir? I'm beyond eating this second roll."

The man's eyes widened and he dropped his burlap bag, the clang of metal stirring Colonel. "Well, I suppose it would be a sin to waste what the good Lord has provided. I am . . . much obliged, sir."

Dickens tossed the man the second roll.

"A nice village, Cornwall?" Dickens asked.

"The people are warm . . . but the winters aren't. The river freezes, sometimes for months." The man broke the end off the hard roll, and the piece of roll disappeared beneath his kerchief. "Still, it has been home for sixty years," the man said, his mouth full.

Dickens offered a generous slice of cheese, which the old man eagerly accepted. "You are too kind, sir." The old man slit the roll with his knife and fitted the cheese inside.

"What takes you to West Point?" Dickens asked.

"I have work there for the next two weeks. Carpentry," the man said, turning his head to one side and pulling the kerchief down around his neck so he could eat the sandwich. "Though I must be back in Cornwall tomorrow for an appointment, which I'm not to miss. An unexpected appointment, but one I'm inclined to make. And I suppose a body cannot have too much exercise."

"I'm headed to Cornwall to call upon one of your own," Dickens said, almost to the man's back.

"Give a name, sir, for doubtless I know him."

"Eben Kruge is the man, an attorney."

The old man turned reflexively, and for an instant exposed the whole of his face, the sight of which evoked a shudder in Dickens. The old man quickly refitted his kerchief.

Not in the hospitals or prisons of London had Dickens ever seen such a scar as scissored across the old man's face from above his right eye to the tip of his chin, transecting nose and mouth, a thick pale lineament on an otherwise tan and agreeable face. Dickens momentarily cursed his power of observation, but then forced a smile. "I have business with him."

"Do you now?" the old man said. "With Kruge?"

The old man's tone was clear.

"Then, you know him?" Dickens asked.

The old man made a show of judging the time. "Well, I . . . really must be going, if I'm to get there. I'm expected midmorning and can't let the gov'ment down." He raised the balance of his sandwich in salute. "But I am indeed in your debt, sir. May God bless you."

Dickens smiled from his high perch, the second bottle of beer in his outstretched hand. "You'll want to wash that down, my friend. Have a pleasant walk and a prosperous day."

As the old man moved on, Dickens corked his bottle of beer, stowed it with the remaining cheese in the small basket, and reached for the reins. Twenty minutes later, he rounded the north face of the behemoth shown on Roe's sketch map as Butter Hill, much more a mountain than a hill, and began a gradual descent to a broad plain stretching northward and eastward to the river bluff. Beyond the plain, he could see the roofline of a village, which according to the map had to be Cornwall. Presently, the road was lined on either side by trees, and to the left, through the trees and a hundred yards up an overgrown incline, catching Dickens's eye, stood a majestic, but ill-maintained house with many gables. Its whitewashed exterior was dulled to a gray finish below its irregular eaves. To the side of the house was a broad clearing.

Chapter Five

Referring to the sketch map, Dickens proceeded a short distance down Cornwall's Main Street, boardwalks on either side, to an intersection and marble obelisk in the center of the road. Beyond the obelisk, on the right, was a white clapboard-sided shop, followed by a single-story red brick structure. On the front of the brick building, above a wooden door, painted black, hung a marquis sign with the lettering *Eben A. Kruge, Esquire* across its middle, and at the bottom, the scales of justice. Above Kruge's name was evidence of another name that had been painted over. The only other feature on the front of the building was a single window; its trim painted black, with four panes, one of which was cracked.

Dickens tethered and watered Colonel at a trough on the opposite side of the street and fed him the bag of oats. Afterwards, he buttoned his waistcoat, donned his topcoat and top hat, fixed his cravat, and crossed the street to the opposite boardwalk. He rapped Kruge's door once, a second time, and then a third time, but received no response. Trying the doorknob, he found it locked. He peered in the window, and from what he could see, the interior of the office was sparsely furnished. He then checked his visage in the window reflection.

"Looking for Mr. Kruge?"

Dickens turned in the direction of the clapboard-sided shop to see a powerfully built black man with close-cropped white hair standing in the doorway of the shop. He took the man, who clinched a pipe in his teeth, to be in his late fifties or early sixties.

"I appear to have missed him," Dickens said.

"Won't be long I'm sure, and you needn't be in the sun." The man motioned for Dickens to come inside. The sign above the man's door read *Jedidiah Micawley, Wheelwright*. Inside the shop and along two walls were workbenches, bundled spokes, and completed wheels, with and without iron rims that hung on pegs about the room. A raw hub was fitted on a lathe, and wood chips and sawdust covered the floor. To Dickens, the room had an altogether pleasing odor. In a corner of the room was a small desk, covered with papers, and next to it a single chair. At the rear of the room was a window and an open door, through which Dickens saw what he took to be a blacksmith shed.

"It's not like Mr. Kruge to absent himself for an appointment," the man said.

"Actually, I come unannounced," Dickens replied. "I'm staying at the West Point Hotel."

The man nodded and extended his hand. "Jedidiah Micawley."

Taking his hand, Dickens introduced himself, "Charles Dickens. And I thank you. It is much cooler in here."

Micawley pulled up a stool. "Please sit. Given your accent, I have to ask . . . any relation to the English writer?"

"That would be me," Dickens said, almost apologetically.

"In Cornwall? To see Kruge?"

"You know Mr. Kruge?"

"I expect everyone here does. Me, since we were grammar school mates."

"And now working in adjacent quarters." Dickens smiled at the thought. "You've been friends a long time?"

"We have . . . known each other a long time." Micawley said, removing the pipe from his mouth. "Do you know Mr. Kruge?"

"No. Not beyond the rumor he is an unusual man and has undergone a change."

Micawley made no reply.

Dickens heard a door close next door.

Micawley gave an acknowledging tilt of his head.

Dickens got to his feet. "I thank you, Mr. Micawley. Your kindness is most appreciated."

Micawley nodded, his pipe back in his mouth.

Dickens knocked once on Kruge's door, and hearing no response let himself in. In the darkness of the office, Dickens waited for his eyes to adjust. When they had, he saw a man with thinning salt and pepper hair and wiry build behind a single desk in the middle of the room. The man was dressed formally in a black suit. The desk faced the entrance, and the man was invested in a document.

"Have I the honor of addressing Mr. Eben Kruge?" Dickens asked.

The bespectacled man raised his eyes from a sheet of parchment and gestured to a leather chair fronting his desk, his eyes returning to the parchment.

Dickens took a seat in a well-worn chair, its cushion collapsing to the extent he could barely see over the top of the desk.

"And who might you be?" Kruge asked in a low, though not unpleasant tone, his eyes still on the parchment.

"Charles Dickens, sir. I am an English writer, and I would like to . . . buy some of your time."

At this, Kruge looked up, producing a face, long and lined, behind thick spectacles, which he removed, revealing eyes, beady and coal black. "Indeed?"

"Yes, for your advice, sir." Having sensed no recognition by Kruge, Dickens asked, "Do . . . you know who I am, sir?"

"You said you are Charles Dickens, and I presume that is who you are."

"Yes, well . . . I am an author. I write stories. And from an international copyright standpoint, being a British author, the fruits of my labor printed in your country benefit me not at all. I receive no royalty and am wholly ignored by your justice . . ."

Kruge raised a finger, "You are offended by our system of justice?"

"By its blindness to international copyright law."

"I was unaware that such law existed, Mr. Dickens, beyond various opinions that it should, and would be a good and just thing if it did."

"Exactly, sir," Dickens said. "Nevertheless, it is not right that piracy be sanctioned across the high seas."

Kruge offered a thin-lipped smile. "And what is it you suppose I can do for you?"

"Well, believing I cannot beat the pirates, I'm reduced to joining them. If your services include framing contracts between a writer and publisher, I would like to know what the basic elements are in your American contracts, as I suspect they are different from our rather lengthy English ones."

Kruge nodded. "Yes . . . likely."

"Then you will help me?"

"I may be able to."

Confidently, quietly, and with an efficiency Dickens found refreshing in an attorney, Kruge proceeded in the span of half an hour to pull books off shelves and documents from drawers to support counsel on the basic elements of American contracts, the more restrictive covenants in contracts between writer and publisher, and what Dickens might want to see in his own contracts.

However, as Kruge practiced his trade, Dickens grew increasingly uncomfortable. He finally cleared his throat, "Mr. Kruge . . . if I may, I should like to ask you a different question."

"Um?" Kruge said, his face in a reference book.

"One . . . unrelated to contracts," Dickens said, deferentially.

Kruge looked up. "What?"

"Sir," Dickens could think of no alternative but to out with it, "it is my understanding that you have experienced something . . ."

Kruge stared at Dickens, his expression unreadable behind his spectacles.

"Sir, that you have had a change of heart," Dickens added quickly.

Kruge lowered the volume he was holding. "I do not understand your meaning, or what it has to do with copyright or contracts. If you please, Mr. Dickens, what is your purpose here?"

"Sir, I have come to . . . inquire about . . . what has happened to you . . . about your story."

Kruge pressed his thin lips together, and returned the volume to the bookcase and himself to his chair. He leaned back, crossed his arms, and cocked his head. "What story?"

"Sir, I am to understand that you have done an about face in all things . . . all things defining your manner and conduct, that . . . the process was quite sudden."

"And your interest in contracts?"

Dickens shook his head. "A shameless ploy, sir. For which I beg pardon."

"But you are going to pay for my services," Kruge said, glancing at the wall clock, "half an hour of my time?"

"Sir, I will pay your full rate, even double it. And I am heartily sorry for the charade. I intended no offense."

Kruge looked askance at Dickens. "But wanted in my door?"

Dickens leaned forward. "Sir, to be candid, as a writer, my stories hang on the characters in them. To date, I've been fortunate. My readers are satisfied; they can't wait for the next installment—to find out what happens to missus good or mister bad, to know how a thing turns out. But the whole hinges on my characters." Dickens paused. "Sir, if I may, have you read any of my works?"

Kruge shook his head. "I've no time for stories, but I do know something of who you are."

"I see . . ." Dickens said, uncertain how to interpret Kruge's response. "Sir, the characters in my stories take readers to where they could never be, for good or ill. My intent, with my characters, the major ones anyway, is that they be larger than the reader, experiencing what they can not, or would not . . . and I perceive you, sir, to be such a . . ."

"Character?" Kruge completed Dickens's sentence in a curt tone.

"I mean no offense, sir."

"You know nothing about me, young man." Kruge picked up a writing quill and swirled it slowly inside his teacup. "How would you like me stirring up your life, Mr. Dickens?"

"Do you deny, sir," Dickens pressed, "an experience so significant that it has transformed you forever, and, I'm to understand, made you a better man?"

"I deny or admit nothing, except that I have a personal life and wish it kept so, not paraded before the world."

"You mistake my purpose, sir. I wish only to know your story, and knowing it create a fiction, a man who might anonymously bear some likeness of you. There is a difference."

"Mr. Dickens, I daresay you have skeletons of the past, perhaps the present, that you are hiding. Am I right?

Dickens was taken by the question. "Sir?"

"Things you've done, said, or experienced that you'd rather not talk about, that you'd prefer secreted from the world?"

Dickens was silent a moment, his eye on the small, intricately carved and well polished miniature wagon wheel on Kruge's desk. The wheel appeared to be made of cherry wood and was affixed to a small granite base bearing a small bronze plate. "I suppose everyone has something . . ."

"Precisely," Kruge said. "And some things should be kept private."

Dickens felt a deflation beyond what he experienced at the Shaker village.

"Of my former life," Kruge continued, "you can know from anyone in Orange County—and it would not be a pleasant education—but you, a total stranger, want me to tell you what I've told no one?"

Dickens did not respond.

"You want to know what happened to me . . . what began the night of Christmas Day last?"

Dickens expected no explanation, and none was forthcoming.

"Mr. Dickens, what is the darkest secret that you hide from the world? The one thing you least want me or anyone else to know. Will you tell me that?"

"Sir, I have no secrets."

"Come now, Mr. Dickens. Everyone has secrets."

"Sir, to my knowledge, I am the most open of men. Nothing constituting life is hid by me from family, friends, or even the public—how can it be otherwise, for I am continually in its eye?"

"So you will not oblige me what I ask, and yet expect me to oblige you?"

At that, Dickens drew himself up. "If you require a secret, let this be mine . . ."

"Yes?" Kruge pressed.

"Picture a childhood destroyed, a father dishonored, and a family disgraced . . . that is what I hide from the world."

Kruge smiled ruefully, "So . . . there it is, there is your secret. But it is safe with me, isn't it? For I am not a writer of stories."

Dickens lowered his eyes.

"Well, Mr. Dickens, what I have not shared with anyone, much less the world, is not of that nature. It is, however, beyond anything you could imagine or should ever want to imagine. I am quite sure of it."

There was a sharp knock on the door, and Kruge glanced at the wall clock. As Kruge rose from his chair, Dickens's heart sank.

"I must beg your pardon, Mr. Dickens. If you wish to talk further, you must come back in an hour. Perhaps you can find amusement in our little town. And do remember the half hour you owe me," Kruge added, perfunctorily. On his feet, Kruge's height surprised Dickens. The old man was easily half a foot taller than himself.

Chapter Six

The man who slipped by Dickens into Kruge's office was small in stature and bore the face of a condemned man. He was dressed shabbily and clutched a worn and faded Dutchmen's cap. He neither responded to Dickens's salutation nor met his eyes. Dickens returned to the buggy and Colonel, and consumed the last of the bottle of beer. He already found the day warm, and thought of the wizened man. The air was still and the street empty except for half a dozen children playing a game that involved kicking an inflated pig bladder. Glancing in the direction he had come, he saw beyond the obelisk the spire of a church.

He stopped to read the inscriptions on the four sides of the obelisk, which commemorated the country's war for independence, and those who had died in its service. One side bore a surface relief of George Washington, and beneath it his various titles and accomplishments. Dickens walked along the shop-lined street in the direction of the church, peering in windows at wares ranging from crockery to hoopskirts. Arriving at the Cornwall Presbyterian Church, he entered the vestibule, and finding no one inside, took a seat on a pew at the back of the sanctuary. Dim light from stained glass windows along the sides of the sanctuary and a single window at the front of the church beneath its eave revealed a simple, even austere interior, the most significant object being a large rustic cross made of wood that hung behind the altar.

There was a metallic creaking sound, and a man entered the sanctuary through a door to the right of the altar. He carried a long-handled shovel as if a musket. The man took notice of Dickens, and after a long stare asked, "May I be of service, sir?"

Dickens stood up. "I don't mean to intrude."

"You are seeking the Reverend?"

"Just a quiet space. Some time to reflect, if that is permissible."

"All the same. Reverend Dean is in New Windsor." The man unshouldered his shovel. "I'll be in the cemetery, if you have a need. A burial this afternoon, and the hole not finished. Just pull the door tight on the way out. The catch is not so good."

Dickens nodded and sat down again. But the man with the shovel spoke once more. "We don't get many visitors here in Cornwall. What brings you, sir?"

"An appointment." Dickens said, eyeing the man's shovel. "You are the sexton?"

"That and all but preacher," the man answered, caressing the shovel. "You know, sir," the man said, as though more conversation was needed, "I find it a rule that the living are more patient than the dead, the dead always being in such a hurry to be buried."

The remark amused Dickens. "Indeed. But I suspect you enjoy your work."

The man stood straight, "I suppose I'm good enough at it." He cocked his head in the direction of the door he had entered. "Judge for yourself and leave through the cemetery. I keep it trim, the place, flowered for color and scent. It's a pretty sight, actually. Everything and everyone in its place."

"As they should be," Dickens said with a grin.

"You said, an appointment?"

"With the man, Eben Kruge. Lawyer business."

The sexton's face suddenly hardened. "Happy the day my spade works for him." And with that, he exited the church.

Alone, Dickens closed his eyes and was soon revisiting his exchange with Kruge. As was his habit, especially when an exchange did not go well, he began to dissect its parts. The ruse he knew could not have been more ill conceived. Why hadn't he simply stated what he wanted and maintained the high ground? He felt certain he'd lost a most remarkable story, for Kruge was even more of a find than he had hoped for.

Worse, Kruge was a man who had undone him, goaded him into admitting the one thing he had kept hid for eighteen years, the one thing that still haunted his inmost being. What had for a lifetime been under lock and key, was unearthed by a flippant challenge from a man he had known less than an hour. No one, not Catherine, not even Forster, knew what the stranger now knew. In the stillness of the sanctuary, he rested his head against the high back of the pew.

Dickens had slept little the night before in anticipation of the day, and the weariness of five months in the fledgling country was bent on its due. Soon consciousness gave way to drowsiness, drowsiness to slumber, and slumber to a dream.

He was again in Chatham, southeast of London and near the coast, eleven years old, the son of a Navy pay office clerk at Chatham's large government dockyard, girded by what he believed to be a splendid childhood, and heading home after school, exhilarated by a day when his words and actions had once again turned the heads of all of his schoolmates and the schoolmaster, Mr. Giles. His chest heaved with the pride of performance.

The years since his fifth birthday had been consistent, full, and, on balance, happy, despite his being frail and small for his age, and in earlier years prone to spasms. Until age nine, the three-story house on Ordnance Terrace had been home, and to him a mansion, and from it he could see all the lower parts of Chatham and the River Medway. Gardens with flowers fronted and backed the house. There were two handsome hawthorn trees, and two female servants stewarded the house and family, his favorite being Mary, who would tell him ghost stories and tales of murder.

At age nine, occasioned by failing family finances, of which he was oblivious, the family moved to St. Mary's Place, known as "the Brook." He took the Brook home in stride, it being a small tenement, but ample enough, with an enchanting attic room that was his, and in which he read voraciously and daydreamed. But as before, he still enjoyed long walks with his father past Gads Hill Place into Rochester or to the countryside, trips to the sea, and occasional trips to London, as well as participating in the filling of frequent invitations to theater and parties to which the whole family went. It was still a happy time—of father, mother, himself, Fanny, his older sister, but only by a year and a few months, and Letitia, Harriett, and Frederick, all younger.

But upon seeing his house, he slowed.

In front of it was a large wagon, and in it, nearly filling it, were articles familiar to him.

He rushed up to a very large man in a much worn tweed coat who was securing the wagon. "Please, sir, what are you doing?"

The large man, with few teeth, turned round. "Doing what I was told to do. That's what I'm doing."

"But you've made a mistake, sir, I'm sure of it. You can't take these things."

"Is this not the residence of one, John Dickens and family?" the man replied, haughtily.

As the wagon departed, he went inside the house, seeking the person he cherished most on earth, a person, to him, the kindest, most generous soul on earth. "Father, what is happening?"

"Not to worry, Charley boy. I have been transferred to London, and we are to live in a new house. Think of it. New friends. An exciting time, Charley."

"But what of the cart, Father? Our dining room table is in it!"

"Charley, it is an old table, and we don't need all the things we have, and can get new ones as we come to know our new lodgings."

He could not know that all in the cart would be sold to pay mounting debts.

"But, Father, what of my schooling?"

"You are to finish the term and stay with the schoolmaster, Mr. Giles. You would like that wouldn't you?"

He didn't answer.

"You are a prodigal, Charley. You know that. You test always at the top of your class. When you join us in the new house, I mean to find you a worthy pursuit to balance your education—the world with the classroom. Perhaps make some money that you might apply to the family, if that is your desire. Then, after a time, we can talk about your going back to school."

"But father . . . I like school, and all my friends are there. And you said, to be a gentleman, I must have an education."

"Charley, you are a gentleman, and never you forget it." The older Dickens's tone, momentarily serious, quickly softened. "Now give me a smile."

But he was unable to smile, and turned quickly on his heels.

From there the dream moved quickly, mirroring the mounting of his father's debts, the unraveling of home, and the fading prospect of ever achieving what he had once taken for granted.

The family next occupied quarters on Bayham Street, in Camden Town, North London, finding it a great disappointment, consisting only of four rooms, a basement, and a garret. And to this confined space was added a sixth child, Alfred. Arriving himself after the fall term of school, he found not a single boy of any age in the neighborhood with whom he wanted to make friends, and thus spent his days despondent, lamenting his losses, doing family errands, watching over younger siblings, and cleaning his father's boots.

His only joy was borrowed books read in his garret space, in which he escaped to far away lands and sundry adventures. But crushed was what had been a propelling prospect voiced more than once by his father when they passed Gads Hill Place, that if he were to work very hard, one day the house there might be his.

From Bayham Street, financial ruin impending, the family moved into an even less agreeable lodging on Gower Street North, and, to his chagrin, only two days after his twelfth birthday, his first employment situation was procured. He was to work, and did work, in a worm-eaten, rat-infested miserable hole of a boot-blacking warehouse from eight in the morning to eight at night, six days a week, tying cloth lids to little bottles of bootblack and gluing on labels. It mattered not to him that he was paid six schillings a week. And while amiable enough, his co-workers he found to be coarse young boys, who cared not a wit for the aspirations of a gentleman or the graces of being one.

And it was upon returning from the warehouse on but the eleventh day of his employment that he saw a black carriage depart from the front of the tenement. Trembling for reasons he knew not, he hesitantly opened the front door. Inside there was no greeting of, "how was your day, Charley?" but only the tear-stained faces of his mother and siblings, all silent around the small dinner table.

"Your father's gone to the Marshalsea," his mother stammered through tears.

"But mother . . ."

"I know, Charley. I know." She drew him close. "That you are man now and working is such a blessing. We are to stay here, Charley, until Father can think of something, or we're told to leave. If we must leave, we will be with Father."

"But . . . be with him where?"

"You are such an innocent, Charley." She stroked his hair. "Be with him in the Marshalsea, in debtors' prison."

Dickens woke sharply from the dream, his brow wet with perspiration. It varied little, the dream, though less distinct with the passage of years. In the space of a day, nay, in the flash of a moment, his life had been changed forever. Never again would there be the blessing of the ordinary, the joy and security of family, the trading of sibling stories over an ample supper, or the sense of a just world. What had been would never be again. The father he had revered, and would continue to love and provide for, had been laid bare for the world to judge, a man disgraced and forever marked as a failure, unable to manage himself or his family, unable to pay his debts, a man bankrupt. And he, Charles Dickens, was that man's oldest son.

Short weeks later, the Gower house was repossessed and all its inhabitants, save himself, were transported to debtors' prison to be with his father. For him, because of his gainful situation, lodging was arranged with an old widow woman, and his days were a blur of unwanted independence, rising very early in the morning, going by himself to the boot-blacking warehouse in every kind of bad weather, and returning to the widow's home for a bite of supper and to fall exhausted in bed. He saw family only on Sundays, until finally, after persistent and tearful pleadings that he be a part of the family, a lodging closer to the detention house was found. The new lodging allowed him to take breakfast and dinner, such as they were, in the Marshalsea and between the two meager meals attend to the daily obligation of tying bottles and pasting labels.

To him, his father's incarceration in the Marshalsea had been a lifetime, though in truth only a few days past three months. His father, after receiving on the death of his mother an inheritance sufficient to satisfy creditors and begin life anew, walked out of the Marshalsea, trailed by his family, a free but much diminished man.

From very frugal quarters, and feeling much older than his twelve years, he once again was allowed to attend school, though against the wishes of his mother who lamented the loss of even six schillings a week, when her husband barely hovered on the correct side of the ledger. As time passed and new associations were made, the shame endured by the family led to a pact, nearly a blood oath and oft renewed, that none would disclose the shame and imprisonment of that year. The word, Marshalsea, was never to cross their lips.

But for him he would never forget the disappointment, privation, and utter sense of abandonment that darkened his eleventh and twelfth years of life. They would haunt him until his dying breath, and indeed had already relived themselves in parts of his writings, and, perhaps, one day might chronicle themselves in a character bearing his own likeness.

The toll of the church bell, sounding eleven o'clock, brought Dickens to the present and to his feet.

Chapter Seven

The small man with the appointment was leaving Kruge's office in the opposite direction when Dickens returned. Dickens knocked once on the door and entered. In the shadows at the back of the large open office, he saw movement. He could see Kruge bent over, closing the lid of what looked to be a trunk.

Seeing the Englishman, Kruge returned to his desk. "So . . . Mr. Dickens."

"I have not paid my bill, sir." Dickens said. "Tell me what I owe, and I will pay it . . . and leave you in peace."

Kruge motioned for Dickens to sit. "Mr. Dickens, would you agree that man is inherently evil?"

The question surprised Dickens, but after reflecting, he answered, "Inherently willful and always prone to sinning and meanness, yes, but not inherently evil." He paused. "Are you a . . ."

"Am I . . . what?" Kruge replied.

"A man of . . . faith?"

"If you mean into religion, I suspect you know the answer to that. Though I have begun to read your book, your Bible."

"Because of last Christmas?"

Kruge studied Dickens. "Partly."

"Have you've gotten to where we, humans, you and I, are made in God's image?"

"I've not read that, but then I was instructed to begin with the second part."

"The New Testament?"

Kruge did not answer, but, rather, posed his own question, "Do you believe in ghosts, Mr. Dickens . . . angels and demons?"

"Why do you ask?"

"If you will, sir, a simple yes or no."

"Yes, there are heavenly beings," Dickens answered, "good and bad."

Kruge eyed Dickens. "And miracles, do you believe in miracles, Mr. Dickens?"

"What do you mean by miracles?" Dickens countered.

"Come now, sir, don't word wrestle with me." There was annoyance in Kruge's tone. "Your Bible is full of them."

"Yes, I believe what is in the Bible."

Kruge tapped his chin. "And in the man, for whom Christmas is named?"

"I do."

"Um," Kruge narrowed his eyes. "And what would you say of me?"

Dickens did not understand the question. "I'm sorry . . . of you . . . what?"

"Whether I believe in miracles."

"All right . . . do you?"

Kruge stroked his rather long chin, and, instead of answering, replied in not much more than a whisper, "So you wish to know my story?"

Dickens wasn't sure he had heard correctly.

"Well, do you?" Kruge said, more audibly.

Dickens was unable to hide his enthusiasm. "I do, sir. Very much so."

Kruge raised a cautionary hand. "Enough to stay the night?"

"Sir . . . ?"

Kruge raised the palm of his hand as if he'd been asked in court to swear on the book in front of him. "What I will tell you, why I am now the man you see before you, you will not believe. Were I you, I would not believe it. I would want proof."

"I do not follow, sir."

"To begin with, my story—the whole of it—is not a short one, but more to the point, evidence of its truth comes only at midnight," Kruge hesitated. "Though I cannot warrant that it comes every midnight."

The instant rush of enthusiasm experienced by Dickens evaporated with Kruge's stipulation. "But I . . . am to be on a steamer at the West Point dock at six o'clock this evening."

"And you still can be." Kruge said, impassively. "It is your decision, Mr. Dickens."

"But you say it may be for naught?"

Kruge's face was unreadable. "What I am saying is that I am not every night where what you will want to see occurs, but when I am, at the stroke of midnight," Kruge's eyes suddenly darted queerly about the room, "it is there. Always there."

Dickens said nothing for a moment, but then wagged a finger at Kruge.

The lawyer leaned back in his chair. "I am only granting what you requested."

Dickens rose from his lowly perch and flashed a wide grin. "Done and done. I will extend my stay. But I must get word back to my wife."

"And now is your chance, as I am expecting . . ."

Kruge was interrupted by three hard knocks on the front door.

Chapter Eight

Dickens opened the door to a tall man, better dressed and comported than the first visitor, though bearing no less anxious a visage. This man, too, ignored Dickens's salutation.

Outside, the day was warmer and more humid, and the smell of horse was heavy in the air.

Seated on a cane chair in front of his store, Jedidiah Micawley called out to Dickens, "Had you a good visit with Mr. Kruge?"

Dickens walked briskly down the boardwalk and pressed his hands together, prayerfully. "Mr. Micawley, I must get a message to West Point, to Captain Roe at the hotel . . . as soon as possible. Can you suggest . . ."

Micawley cut him short. "My grandson, James, will take your message, and do so on my horse. Neither has done anything constructive in days. James will have it there in less than an hour. With school out, he needs something gainful. He's just there." Micawley rose to his feet and pointed to one of the several boys in the street kicking the pig bladder.

Dickens expressed relief by shaking Micawley's hand vigorously. "And I will make it worth his while." Dickens exclaimed. "Now I must pen a note."

"Which you may do in my office. Quill, ink, and vellum are on the desk. I'll fetch young James."

Dickens sat at Moore's desk, the quill in his fingers scratching across the paper.

> *Captain Roe, No time to explain. All is well. However, must stay the night in Cornwall—return tomorrow in time for last boat. Assure Catherine, and, if not engaged, please invite her to dine. She will cherish your company. Beholden, Chas Dickens*

Dickens folded the sheet twice, and glanced with curiosity at what was on the corner of Micawley's desk. When he emerged from the wheelwright's store, a youth atop a sorrel mare stared down at him, apprehensively.

"You must be James, my courier," Dickens said officiously, which produced a sudden swelling of the boy's chest.

"James is my youngest grandson, and likely my best in the saddle." Micawley turned to his grandson. "Listen well to what Mr. Dickens says to you."

Dickens handed the note to the boy. "How old are you, James?"

"Eleven, sir, this past month."

"An easy task for an eleven-year-old, James," Dickens said with a smile. "I just want you to tell the guard at West Point you have an important message for Captain Roe at the hotel and must deliver it right away." Dickens handed James the note. "Can you do that, James?"

"Captain Roe, at the hotel. Yes, sir." The boy slipped the note inside his shirt. Dickens pressed a coin in the palm of the boy's hand, and the boy examined it, his eyes expanding with the sight. "Look, Grandpa!" The boy held up the gold coin.

"Well, would you look at that . . . an American Half Eagle, that one!" Micawley said approvingly, glancing at Dickens. "Alright then, off with you. James!"

Without another word, the horse and boy were off, Dickens and Micawley watching until they were out of sight.

Returning to the wheelwright shop, Micawley excused himself and returned with a cup of cool water for Dickens. As Dickens drank, Micawley rephrased his earlier question, "What did you think of our Eben Kruge?"

"I think I know very little of him," Dickens replied. "On surface, cordial enough, but I suspect he goes much deeper."

"Yes, like icebergs do," Micawley observed. "Hard and cold."

Dickens considered Micawley's response, but let it pass. "Tell me, sir, about your family, how you came to be . . ." Dickens hesitated.

"A black wheelwright?" Micawley offered, drawing a smile and a nod from Dickens.

"I've seen a lot of your country and your race," Dickens said. "And to be candid, the Negro is sorely treated throughout most of it. But here, you are a wheelwright, a craft mastered by few, regardless of race."

"It is hard work to be sure," Micawley agreed, "requiring a good eye, a sense for wood, and strength to work and fit the many pieces in a wheel, and to smith iron and set a rim."

"And you decided . . . just to do it?"

"After apprenticing with my father, who apprenticed with the Army during the war . . . the first one with you British . . . no offense." Micawley said.

Dickens smiled.

"At the beginning of the war, he was doing livery work in Washington's Army. He knew horses better than most. But soon enough they were looking for volunteers to learn how to repair and make wheels. My father raised his hand when nobody else did, and was set to learning the trade in the quartermaster corps. Soon he was fixing and making wheels for wagons, carriages, and artillery pieces, whatever was needed. And, as a man half again my size, he was good at it. After Yorktown and the war, he jobbed as a wheelwright in Newburgh, and near the turn of the century set up his own shop here in Cornwall, having received an unexpected bequest."

"So never a slave?" Dickens asked.

"Not him, but his father, my grandfather, who himself was freed when his master died."

"Tell me there's not a story there," Dickens said.

"A lot of injustice in the world, Mr. Dickens," Micawley said, reflectively. "Injustice that's got nothing to do with slavery."

"And your family?"

"I've had a good life, Mr. Dickens, a lot of joys, but, as all of us, my share of trials and sadness."

"Children?" Dickens asked.

"Well, how else would young James be here?" Micawley said with a weak smile. "Four boys and two girls, Millie and I had. All but three died in infancy . . . each breaking Millie's heart."

"I'm sorry to know it, sir," Dickens said in sympathy.

"They are in heaven now, and without pain, and I believe we will see them soon enough."

"And James's parents?" Dickens asked.

Micawley looked away for a moment. "James is a junior. His father, our oldest, and his wife died from small pox five years ago. Millie and I take care of James. His two older brothers are off to sea. We get occasional letters from them, each in a different ocean, but haven't seen either since they left." Micawley forced a smile. "Our two girls are both married with families in New York City."

Dickens pointed to what was on Micawley's desk. "That wheel, quite detailed . . . you carved and painted it yourself?"

"I did," he said good-naturedly. "Evidence, I suppose, of too much idle time."

"There is one like it on Mr. Kruge's desk."

"An earlier gift," Micawley said, his face unreadable. "You are staying the night?"

"I am."

"Because of Kruge?"

"You are not fond of the man, are you? With such history and proximity . . . I would have thought otherwise."

"There are things you don't know, Mr. Dickens. But I'll not say more of it. You should form you own opinions."

"You saw the man that last went into Kruge's office?"

"I did."

"Do you know him?"

"He is from New Windsor, north of here."

"He seemed much agitated."

"And with reason."

"How so . . . ?"

"I believe that is between him and Mr. Kruge."

"Fair enough, but answer me this . . . have you observed a recent and rather remarkable change in Kruge?"

"I have . . ."

"For the good."

"It would appear so."

"Since when, if you can remember?"

"How can I forget? It was this past Easter. I remember it, because it was then, or maybe the day after, that he asked me about the Bible."

"The Bible?"

"You cannot know how unlike Kruge such a question would be," Micawley said, his face inscrutable. Anyway, I suppose you'll be needing a place to stay, and if you don't mind a bit of sawdust, I can make you up a pallet. And I expect you'll be needing a livery."

Chapter Nine

Leaving the wheelwright's shop, Dickens followed Micawley's directions to the livery, and left Colonel and the hotel buggy in its care. It was a quarter past noon when he returned to Kruge's office and knocked on the door.

Kruge looked up from his desk. "Mr. Dickens, perhaps you would join me for a midday meal. I have it delivered daily, and that will give us a chance to talk."

"I should like that very much, sir," Dickens said.

"Make yourself comfortable." Kruge rose to his feet and retreated to the back of the room. It appeared to Dickens that Kruge was opening the same trunk he had closed earlier. When Kruge returned, what he carried he kept hidden behind his back. "If you will turn your head, please."

Dickens did so, and Kruge placed three objects on the floor beside his chair.

"You may turn around," Kruge said, again seated. "So, then, Mr. Dickens, about me. I was born in 1783, a child you might say of the revolution. My father, Eben Lloyd Kruge, fought a year in the revolution against your people, met and married my mother when he was sixteen and she but fourteen, and I was born a year later, or maybe less. The fighting done, my father became a whaler and my mother took in cleaning. We lived, I do not know precisely where, but shared a flat with my mother's mother in Newburgh, north of here; she being a widow. When I'm three years old, my father and all the crew of his ship are lost at sea. Gone. Vanished. My mother said a nor'easter had taken them. In truth, I have no memory of him, but I do have this."

Kruge placed a small hand-whittled, wooden boat on his desk.

"Mother told me father made it, and she gave it to me after he last left."

Kruge handed Dickens the boat, and Dickens made a show of admiring it, though in truth he found it crude, with a stubby mast that in earlier life had been a chair spindle.

"The color is my own, added later," Kruge said, with evident pride. "I used my school paints, and I want to assure you that I had as many hours of delight captaining this boat and its travels, as if it had been a thing artfully crafted. And, certain, it floats as well as any boat might."

Dickens nodded and placed the boat on the desk.

Following a light tap on the door, a stout buxom woman entered with a cloth-covered tray.

"Just there, Helga." Kruge pointed to the low table beside Dickens. "And I'll be sharing with the gentleman. I'll use my tea cup." The woman complied in silence, uncovering the tray, which included a plate of sausages, sliced cucumber, green olives, a saucer of brown mustard, two thick slices of brown bread, a bottle of beer, a ceramic stein, and cutlery. She poured the beer in Kruge's cup and then in the stein for Dickens, and excused herself.

"Would you mind putting some mustard and a sausage on a piece of that bread," Kruge asked. "That will do me, and the rest is for you."

Dickens did as requested, and then raised his stein. "Your health, sir."

"And yours," Kruge tipped his cup. "So, when my father was gone, we lived with my grandmother—we called her, Nana—until I was eight. I started school when five, and all was well enough until Nana passed. Mother was never a healthy woman, and I think the loss of my father and then her mother was beyond her bearing. She could not hold a job, and we soon had no money. And it was then that my uncle, two years mother's senior, took us in, he a bachelor and a lawyer and banker of sorts here in Cornwall, his name, Hans Gerber Roth."

"A good man?" Dickens asked.

"Prone to drink, and always too much. And when he did, he'd curse the world, though mostly me—me feeling the belt often enough. Mother was always to my defense, and when she was, he would curse her, too. Then, when I am eleven, mother takes a fever . . . a very bad fever." Kruge cleared his throat. "In a week, she is delirious and knows me not. Then she is gone . . . and a week later my uncle gives me this."

Kruge placed a tarnished bronze candlestick on the desk, and with his finger gingerly traced its profile.

"The only thing in the whole wide world my mother owned."

Dickens nodded in silence.

"So then it is just my uncle and me. One evening he calls me down for a counsel, before he gets seriously into his cups. That's what he'd call it, a counsel. When he thought it time to tell me how it was going to be; he'd say, 'Eben, you and me, we are going to have a counsel.'"

Kruge sipped his beer.

"By then," Kruge continued, "I have been in Cornwall grammar school maybe three years, have made some close friends, two in particular. But sitting nose to nose with me, he tells me that I am no longer on the take, but must earn my way for the privilege of going to school and for the right of his room and board. He says I am at all times to be invisible to him, except to do what chores he assigns, and it is to be this way until the day I bless him by leaving his house."

"Then, a hard and cruel man."

"I felt so at first, and always loathed him. But time passes and in a few years, I perceive a kind of wisdom in the man, or so I took it, and would think my life long, until this past Christmas."

Kruge placed the candlestick on the floor, and replaced it with a small copper chest, eight inches square and four inches high, with a latch and key. He unlocked the latch and raised the lid. He tilted the box so that Dickens could see inside.

"What do you see?"

"A box. An empty box."

"Yes, but it was often quite full. And here, Mr. Dickens, you should ask me what chores I did for my uncle?"

"Then I do."

"Everything about the house, of course, and for it received nothing, except the right live in it. But soon I become indispensible to the old troll, though in those days he was only in his early thirties. I become his collections boy for rents and loan payments, running in every direction after school and on weekends to receive his due from those under his boot. And it was for this purpose he gave me the chest, in which I was to place what was owed him. I was his henchman, and for this he a paid me a stipend from what I brought in."

"And you are how old?"

"No more than eleven when I make my first collection. But I was big for my age, and he spared me no pain in training me up for the task, how to speak and not to smile, how never to show pity, that pity was weakness. From the beginning, I was astounded at how those who owed my uncle curried my favor, making their deposits in the box with rubbery faces, inquiring about my uncle's health, insisting that I give him their best."

Kruge drummed the empty chest with a pencil.

"And, of course, there were those, though not so many, who could not pay what was due, or could not pay all that was due. They would beg me, a mere boy, often with tears, to take their storied excuses back to my uncle, with promises that payment would be made as soon as possible."

Kruge swirled the pencil around the interior of the chest.

"An empty chest never sat well with uncle. To him, a deal was a deal, and terms were terms, no matter how poorly struck by one of the parties. And many was the time when a poor creature was stripped of possessions, put in prison, or worse, to settle a debt—something of which you obviously know."

Dickens ignored the inference. “Yours was an intolerable childhood, Mr. Kruge. And for it, I am heartily sorry.”

“The past is past,” Kruge said. “And in our unpleasant common ground, we have a kind of connection, don’t we? Though,” Kruge shrugged his shoulders, “unlike you, I perceive, I did not lament its loss. Rather, I accepted life on the terms presented, and invested myself in living it to my best advantage. The result being that I eventually became more of my uncle than he was of himself.”

“And what of your uncle, now?” Dickens asked, knowing the answer.

“Dead this past Christmas Eve day, though suffering his final four years from a parasitic disorder, an infestation of the flesh . . . something that slowly . . . ate up his body.”

Dickens found himself wincing.

“It wasn’t leprosy,” Kruge said. “But the effect was the same. A very nasty business, and he was boxed and buried the next day, Christmas day. That was his wish, and I obliged it.”

“So you have always been . . . with your uncle?”

“Nay, Sir!” Kruge said emphatically. “When I was just fifteen, tall for my age, and with the appearance of a grown man, and having grown a pretty mustache and accumulated earnings sufficient for my expenses, I fled him and Cornwall to Columbia University, which before the war was your King’s College.”

“Then you escaped your uncle?”

“For a time. After college, I attended law school, and at the end of my year of law, when I’m all intentioned to lawyer in New York City with a firm that has made me a fine offer, I get a letter from the miserable rat.”

“I don’t follow.”

“The man whose boot is on me as much as all his clients wants me to come partner with him, to share equally in the income, and to inherit his trade, declaring that I was much suited to it, and he would one day leave it to me.”

“So you partnered with your uncle?”

“That surprises you,” Kruge said, “the man I would have gladly smothered in his sleep, had I the courage as a boy? No, I did not. At least not at first.”

“But eventually?” Dickens pressed.

“Are we not, all of us,” Kruge said, “at times dogs that return to our mess. And shall I tell you of the fortune I have amassed in his corner?” Kruge laughed aloud, and for the first time in Dickens’s hearing, the roughness of it evincing its rare appearance.

A hard knock on the door brought the conversation and the meal to an end.

Chapter Ten

Dickens was surprised when he left Kruge's office to see that it had been a short, slightly built, elderly woman dressed in widow's black who had done the knocking. But she carried herself with stateliness that impressed Dickens, and took him aback with eye contact and an offered nod.

Dickens walked down the boardwalk to the wheelwright shop, to find on the door a note. *Gone to Lunch.* Dickens looked about, and across the street saw a woman in full-length calico, wide-brimmed hat, and carrying a parasol. She was peering in the window of a cutlery shop.

Dickens approached the woman, who was comely and in her early twenties. He bowed. "I beg your pardon, ma'am, but where would one likely take a midday meal in Cornwall?"

The woman eyed Dickens's dress and smiled. "Granger's, I suppose. Mind you a meal at home will cost you much less. But from your accent, I suppose home is far away. Granger's is a left at that tallish thing in the intersection, and then two blocks toward the river, on your left. The fish will be best."

Dickens thanked the woman and proceeded as directed. Seated by the window in the small eatery, with only three other patrons present, was Micawley.

Micawley smiled and motioned Dickens to take a chair.

"Stalking me?" Micawley said, nearly done with a plate of fish and chips. "Millie is with her mother until evening, so I thought I'd treat myself. The fish is excellent."

A teenage girl in a white blouse, long skirt and apron came to the table, and in a lilting voice announced, "Hi there. My name's Nan, and today's special is what Mr. Micawley's having, fish and chips, and the fish is a fine shad. Dessert is a peach cobbler. That and a drink all for a dollar."

Dickens smiled. "You make it sound delicious, young lady, but just a glass of cider, please."

By the time the girl returned with the cider, Micawley was done with his meal.

"So Eben Kruge was a mean one," Dickens said, more as a question.

"Despised, insufferable, loathed, hated," Micawley replied, half smiling. "Any would fit the bill for Kruge, though more so his uncle."

"All of which Kruge freely admits," Dickens said. "He has been most candid."

Micawley nodded, pensively. "Yet as a child, we the same age, he was as good and as bad as the rest of us. No different. It was his uncle that poisoned him."

Dickens ran a finger around the rim of his mug. "The three visitors that Kruge received today, you knew the one. How about the other two?"

"Didn't see the others. But likely as not, I'd know them."

"All from Cornwall?"

"None from Cornwall, I should think. With few exceptions, Kruge and his uncle were not inclined to foul their own nest. The gentleman I saw, the tall one, I told you was from New Windsor, but Kruge and his uncle worked their will all about Orange County—Goshen, Bloomingburg, Gibralter, Salisbury, Middletown, Newburgh, and as far south as Warwick—oh, and across the river in Fishkill. And I've no reason to doubt elsewhere."

"And just what was their trade?"

"On the surface, legal work. All sorts of civil matters. But, beneath the surface, shysters; moneylenders packaging usury. Always perched on a high branch, looking for prey, with the vulture's code of ethics—the old, the ignorant, the desperate—all fair game. In that, they played no favorites. Though, three years ago, his uncle had to quit the game, unable to fly."

"So they would lend money . . . ?"

"Take the tall man that visited Kruge this morning. Since it is common knowledge, I suppose I can tell you. He had a lumber business, a fine business and doing well. Maybe ten years ago, he wants to expand it. For that he needs capital, and a lot of it. Kruge's uncle suggests, instead of a traditional loan, which would require a high interest rate, that the tall man consider a non-controlling investor. Now that would catch you off guard, wouldn't it?" Micawley gave a rueful smile. "The uncle allows that he would make the investment, and require only a twenty percent share of the profits, and for it would need a forty-nine percent interest in the company. The deal is struck, but before the ink is dry, Kruge's uncle calls a company meeting and declares that he has just purchased the two percent interest of the tall man's grandfather, whose mind and body are nearly gone. Announcing his now controlling ownership, the uncle reduces the tall man to a menial position in management, and takes over the company himself. And you can imagine how it goes. Kruge's uncle takes a handsome salary, shares it with Kruge, I'm sure, and ignores the opinions and recommendations of those who understand the business. The tall man's expansion plans are never realized, and in three years fifty percent of the work force is gone."

"And now?"

"The company lost most of its market years ago to a company started by those who left. The tall man was put back as senior manager three years ago, but I fear too late."

"And this is common knowledge?"

"Cornwall is a tight town, and it and the surrounding villages are a tight community. What happens gets known quickly enough. Especially, when it involves Kruge and his uncle."

"What about you and Kruge, how is it between you two?"

Micawley smiled again. "Allow me to be consistent, and not answer that question."

"You are consistent, but so am I," Dickens smiled. "Tell me, are you aware of any unusual happenings in Cornwall or its surroundings?"

"Why do you ask?"

"Just curious, what with stories and legends that come from this area."

"Mostly Dutch fairytales you're thinking of, but I for one would not want to find myself after hours in the dark wood."

"The dark wood?" Dickens said.

"Coming from West Point, you would have passed through dense woods coming round Butter Hill, some of the trees quite tall."

Dickens said that he had.

"South and west of here on Schunemunk Mountain, the highest mountain in Orange County, there is an expansive stand of trees three times the height of any you might have seen on Butter Hill. They are large diameter trees that grow close together, their tops forming one crown that blocks the sun . . . always."

"The dark wood?"

Micawley nodded. "And every few years, somebody goes missing from around here, and the thought is that they are lost to the dark wood."

"When was the last?"

"A year ago, a girl of twelve. And it's always a girl or a woman, never a male."

"And you believe they are taken to that mountain."

"Taken or lured."

"You don't seem to be a man of fantasy, Mr. Micawley."

"I don't believe it to be fantasy, Mr. Dickens."

"Why do you say that?"

"I . . . have been there. Not at night, mind you," Micawley spoke in a low tone, since the young girl was clearing a table nearby. "But when I was a boy, the age of James, two friends, my best friends, the three of us saw the dark wood for ourselves."

"Tell me . . ."

"Nearly fifty years ago, it was. We three at school on a fall morning, very cold it was, all of us regretting what we'd accepted the day before, from who, I can't even remember now. It was a dare, a simple dare, that we find the dark wood and bring back proof we had. None of us let on what we think of the dare, so much face to save, even that young. When we arrive at the schoolhouse, instead of going in, we set off with vittles in kerchiefs, headed more or less southwest to Schunemunk Mountain, where most folks thought the dark wood to be. Legend had it that the Lenni Lenape Indians, a matriarchal tribe, had a village up on the mountain. We understood that after the Revolutionary War, the tribe was taken to reservations, and had no reason to believe otherwise. Anyway, we strike out, the three of us, eleven years old, afraid of nothing."

The young girl cleared their table.

"We have no plan, of course. We figure just to make our way as best we can to the mountain, and once on top look around for big trees. That simple. It's more miles than we figure, and nearly noon when we finally summit Schunemunk, a majestic piece of earth. I figure we've walked at least ten miles." Micawley sipped his beer. "So, once there, we each climb a tree, looking for the big trees, and I am the one who sees them first!" Micawley voice held childish enthusiasm. "Giant trees, Mr. Dickens! Biggest trees I'd ever seen, and as close as they seemed, it was half an hour before we got to them. And when we get there and are inside, beneath the crown, it is the darkest dark you could ever imagine in daytime."

"Extraordinary," Dickens said.

"I see it as plain as yesterday, and smell it too. A humus odor, the pine needles and earth, soft as sponge, and not a breath of wind, not the faintest sound . . . only the three of us, our breathing. A silver moss coated everything wood . . . and I had a branch, shaped like a walking stick. It was to be my proof. We are sitting on a log resting, finishing what we had to eat. Daniel was dividing an apple. I remember being so thirsty. And that's when I first heard it. We all did."

"Heard what?"

"The sound, like singing, quiet at first, like maybe a lullaby . . . I still hear it sometimes in my dreams. There were words, female voices, I think, but nothing I can understand. It was beautiful, haunting music, but, sudden-like, it gets louder—much louder." Micawley hesitated.

"Try to remember," Dickens urged, "This is fascinating."

"I don't know . . . the noise seemed to press in on us, it was more than just sound."

"Could you see anything?" Dickens interrupted.

"Nothing, just the trees. But I know it's all around us, and so close. We all thought the same thing. We had to get away."

Micawley's voice was anxious.

"I run so fast my feet never touch the ground. And I realize I've left my staff, my proof. But there was a scream . . . behind me. The most dreadful sound I have ever heard, before or since, and I never look back." Micawley looked at Dickens. "Sir, I didn't stop until I was off the mountain, not until I was at the stream we crossed. When I reach it, I'm on all fours drinking like a dog. So thirsty."

"And the others?"

"It's maybe ten minutes, and I'm thinking the worst . . . what am I to tell everyone . . . but then I see them . . . I see Daniel." Micawley involuntarily shuddered.

"Are you alright, sir?" Dickens asked.

Micawley didn't respond.

"Sir, you are to be congratulated, for you are a born storyteller," Dickens quipped, wanting to ease Micawley's anxiety. "And I hope you have no plans to move to England."

"None of us has any proof," Micawley said, almost in a whisper. "We lose the dare . . . though some believed . . . because of Daniel."

"The scream?" Dickens pressed.

Micawley turned to Dickens. "What you should be asking is who the other boy was."

Dickens considered, and gave Micawley a look of disbelief. Micawley nodded his head. "That's right. Eben Kruge."

"How does that happen?"

Micawley glanced at the wall clock, and was quick to his feet. "I must be off. I haven't trimmed the Johnson's wheel, and it's already two o'clock."

Leaving Granger's, Dickens and Micawley returned to Main Street, and as they walked, Dickens asked, "The wheel on the granite base in Kruge's office, you have one just like it. And there is the same brass plate. Am I permitted to ask the connection?"

"For reasons you need not know, Kruge would periodically come to my shop and look around. Mind you, Kruge is a much different person now, not the person I knew as a kid."

"Understand."

"About a year and a half ago, the day before Christmas, if I recall rightly. He is in my shop and we are having a discussion . . . and, shall we say, it grows heated, and during the whole, he is looking at one of the wheels that I've carved, painted, and mounted. *Wheels West* is what I engraved on the brass plate, honoring the Conestoga wagon, which expanded our colonies, and took us west. I can't tell you how many of the full-size wheels I've made and repaired. Anyway, I am suddenly caught up in the season to give up my argument, but not until I swear an oath against Kruge."

"You, an oath . . . ?"

"You don't know the circumstances," Micawley said. "But I realize what I've done, and told Kruge I am sorry, which I attempt to be, though I can tell you it is an uncommon hard thing to do or to be with him. Anyway, I retracted the oath and begged his forgiveness. After sleeping on it, the next day I knock on his door and present him one of the wheels. A peace offering."

"An expensive one, I should think." Dickens said. "And did he . . . forgive you?"

Micawley shook his head.

Chapter Eleven

Returning to Kruge's office, Dickens encountered on the boardwalk the woman in black widow's garb, and tipped his hat. As the two passed, the woman spoke, almost under her breath, "I suppose you received the same treatment?"

Dickens turned.

The woman waited for an answer, and when she didn't receive it, spoke again, "Wasn't that you leaving Kruge's office?"

"It was," Dickens said.

"Then I suppose he set you up, as he did me?"

Dickens sensed an opportunity to learn something. "I expect he did."

"But how did an Englishman get snared in his trap?"

"You Americans don't have a lock on bad judgment," Dickens replied, drawing a smile from the woman. "How did it go with you?"

The woman gave him a look. "Now, I can't tell you that, can I? Same as you can't tell me." She opened her parasol to shield the sun. "Anyway, we'll find out soon enough, won't we?"

"I'm sure we will," Dickens replied.

A moment later, Dickens was in Kruge's office, selecting a stiff, cane-backed chair to sit on.

"With the interruptions," Kruge began, "are you not becoming bored with our little town?"

"Actually, I've been spending time with your neighbor, Mr. Micawley." Dickens said.

"Micawley?" Kruge said lightly, expressing no emotion, save a single nod of the head. After glancing at the rear of the office, he gave Dickens a pensive look. "I should share with you one more thing that defines me—before and after I came to partner with my uncle."

"Please," Dickens said, intrigued.

"There was a space of a year after I graduated from law school, when I took the offer with the firm in New York City—an established firm, quite reputable, with nearly thirty attorneys. I worked hard, and was recognized for my work. One of the senior partners, a former Englishman, quite distinguished actually, had a daughter, her name was Abigail," Kruge paused, "a very pretty girl, outside and in, and . . . I courted her, and soon came to fall in love with her."

Dickens could not hide his surprise.

"And she me," Kruge affirmed. "I proposed to her with her parent's blessings, and we were engaged to be married. I spent many weekends as a guest at the family estate. Her father was a golfer, had played golf in England, and was quite fond of the game." Kruge looked at Dickens. "Do you play golf, Mr. Dickens?"

"No, sorry. Never the time."

"Her father had cleared a large piece of land and made himself three holes of golf. And he was insistent I learn the game, that one day it would catch on in America. So I did, and I paid close attention, practiced, and became quite good at it, actually. After some months, I found I could beat him, but, of course, was wise enough not to." Kruge glanced out the window. "Abigail was delighted. She would carry my three clubs and squeal with delight with my every shot, even the bad ones." Kruge forced a smile. "She was so much fun. The happiest days of my life . . ."

Kruge had to clear his throat.

"A month before we are to wed, she contracts small pox—there is nothing to be done. It is winter, a harsh one, and she does not survive. My Abigail is gone. She is only eighteen."

"Mr. Kruge," Dickens said, greatly moved, and thinking of Mary, his deceased sister-in-law. "I am so sorry."

It was a moment before Kruge could collect himself. "I suppose you would say she was a woman of great faith. And with it she infected me. Wittingly or not, she had changed me into a weaker man, one unprepared to deal with the harshness, the reality of life . . . with her death. At her funeral, I vowed to return to the sanctum of my former self, to rebuild my shield against the world. But it was a slow thing coming, and might never have come, had I not received another of my uncle's persistent letters. Unable to bear my loss, and in a workplace where I saw her father daily, each encounter freshening the wound, I acted upon the letter . . ."

"And became his partner," Dickens said.

"Yes."

"Your age?"

"By then, twenty or twenty-one," Kruge replied, shifting in his chair. "But returning to you, Mr. Dickens, and your secret. Am I to believe that, otherwise, fate has given you no regrets, treated you well for . . . how many years?"

"Thirty years, sir." Dickens replied.

"I would have thought younger," Kruge said, "but then having no beard or mustache promotes a youthful appearance."

"And, for me, that may change, as the thought of a mustache is beginning to have its appeal. Though," he added with a smile, "It must be agreeable to the wife and not frighten the children."

"A loving wife and children . . . I envy your life, your pleasures," Kruge said, wistfully.

"But not without its twists," Dickens said. "After my father was released from debtors' prison, I was back in school. But three years later, we are again evicted from our home. I take a job as a clerk in a law firm, later learning shorthand and becoming a freelance court reporter at the Doctors' Commons. And to this day, I find myself supporting both parents and siblings."

"Indeed, that must be a burden," Kruge mused. "But at least, in such, it is only your purse that suffers."

"There's more." Dickens offered, recalling his first love, Maria Beadnell. "While not a secret, for I was as public and brash about it as a man of eighteen can be, Catherine, the woman I have married and whom I love, is not my first love, and she knows and accepts it." Dickens glanced at the window. "My first love was a girl two years my senior . . . beyond beautiful, and able to excite in me all things romantic. She was the essence of all that I saw in a future wife . . . delicate, charming, witty, and able to affect my every mood with a smile, laugh, frown, or tear. But I was an unknown to her father, a banker, who viewed me as being without serious prospects. Still, I called upon her for more than two years, intent on making her my wife . . ."

"And?" Kruge pressed.

"I was never able to sway her father, or, in truth, seriously win her affection."

"How ended it?" Kruge asked.

"She lost interest in me and broke my heart . . . beyond mending, and at some point was sent off to Paris to a finishing school, later marrying a sawmill manager." Dickens forced a smile. "My pride a shambles, I believed myself incapable of loving again, but . . . apparently time does salve all wounds."

Kruge nodded, responding in a whisper, "One can hope."

"And you sir," Dickens asked, intent on changing the subject, "what did you do for your uncle?"

"Like every apprentice," Kruge replied, easily, "I learned the trade—one you would call contemptible—as I do now—but one with bounds. For you see, my uncle had a curious ethic, which I came to embrace. He might rob you blind, legally, and without remorse, but if he saw you in a bar leave your gold watch on the counter, he would let you know it."

"Then you and he were honest in your dealings?" Dickens asked.

"Quickly enough, as did my uncle, I saw myself not as evil or bad, but as shrewd, for my clients and myself. I have always been content to work within the bounds of the law—my uncle, as well. Not for the righteousness of the law, but for the opportunities afforded by it. For, often as not, the law is neither just nor right, it just is, and once understood can be used to great advantage. The law is a human device, a wonderful labyrinth for those who understand it, how to manipulate it, and can distance themselves from the effects its application has on their fellow creatures."

Kruge paused, and off the expression on Dickens's face added, "Mr. Dickens, in the world there is misery, yes? It is our history and fate. It comes to all of us—to some by circumstance, to some from those meaning harm, and to some even from well-intentioned friends, but in the mix is that which comes from decisions we make, for which we must take responsibility. Tell me, sir, in a business deal, are not the parties to it, who sign the contract, bound by the contract?"

Dickens nodded, reluctantly, remembering how his previous publisher had duped him, using their contract as a defense.

Kruge stared at Dickens for a long moment, and then opened a side drawer. He produced a thick black, leather-bound book.

"A Bible?" Dickens said, more than surprised to see it.

"You've read it through?" Kruge asked.

"Yes. Much of it many times."

"And so I ask you as before, you believe what is in it?"

"I do."

"All of it?"

"It is not a buffet."

Kruge smiled.

Dickens motioned with his eyes to the leather-bound book. "Do you have a problem with something?"

"Something?" Kruge attempted a chuckle as he got up from his desk.

Dickens watched Kruge pace back and forth behind the desk, his chin in his hand. Suddenly Kruge turned to him, thrusting his finger at the Bible. "Virgin birth, water into wine, feeding thousands with two fish, chasing off demons, giving sight to blind people, legs to cripples, curing lepers, walking on water, raising dead people," Kruge spoke as if to a jury things preposterous. "Can these things really be, Mr. Dickens?"

"You miss the point, sir," Dickens said evenly, "though the miracles were witnessed, often by many people—sometimes thousands."

"Then what is the point, Mr. Dickens?" Kruge asked, taking his seat. "What is the purpose of the book?"

"That God has a plan for humankind, that though we stray from it, he has given us a way back."

"Your man from Galilee?" Kruge replied, facetiously.

"It's a matter of faith, Mr. Kruge. What your Abigail had."

Kruge returned the Bible to the drawer, "Seems to me your Galilean picked some very weak people to follow him."

Dickens ignored the remark. "I hope you continue your reading, sir."

"Um," Kruge said, equivocally. "Now about my darker side . . . though I will not belabor it, as I quickly became the twin of my uncle, and have remained consistent these too many years until this Christmas past." Kruge produced from a second drawer several folders, arranging them on his desk. "In these are facts and figures attesting to the ill I've authored or co-authored since I returned to Cornwall." Kruge opened one, took a moment to refresh his memory and raised his eyes. "Here we have owners of a fine home—you might say a mansion—and you likely saw it coming into town from the south, off to the left, up the hill."

"I did," Dickens said. "A fine looking structure, though in need of freshening, I should think."

"Do tell," Kruge said, his eyes narrowed. "For it is my home now, and has been since . . ." Kruge referred to the ledger, "the summer of '22. And I suppose you're right about upkeep, and I suppose I can afford to tear it down and rebuild it ten times over. But it suits me as it is. And, though unkempt now, on the property are two holes for golf, which I designed myself. For a time, I played the two holes daily, pretending my Abigail was beside me, cheering my good shots . . ." Kruge selected another ledger, and recounted how he and his uncle had taken advantage of a spinster and her wealth. And so Kruge continued.

When he perceived Kruge finished, Dickens nodded his head. "I was hoping otherwise, Mr. Kruge, but you have spoken true. You are, or were, more than . . . despicable."

"Yes. And should I tell you of two winters ago, mid December, when my uncle is bedridden, with no mind for business, and little mind otherwise. I must take sole credit for this one—a matter strictly of business. I am, of course, the richest, most powerful man within twenty miles of Cornwall. It is a harsh winter, the river frozen over early. Provisions of foodstuffs, heating oil, and the like are under stocked in Orange County. Most of what there is, I own or control, for I see it coming. And what do you suppose I do with that situation, Mr. Dickens?"

"Nothing good, sir."

"Expect no quarter, give no quarter," Kruge said. "I priced my goods twice, sometimes thrice the going rate. Supply and demand, nothing sinister to my mind, at least not then."

"With no compunction whatsoever for those who could not pay, and might not survive otherwise?" Dickens said.

Kruge shrugged his shoulders. "My prices were paid, and to my knowledge no one froze in the dark." Kruge gathered up the legers. "And so, there you have a piece of it, and that is who I was . . . Eben Kruge, the illegitimate offspring of his uncle's avarice. But I am very sorry for it now, and I am no longer that man." Kruge glanced at the wall clock and sprang to his feet.

"Now I must admit to an appointment I have in Newburgh, a town just three miles up river, past New Windsor. And while I know it will be inconvenient for you, I want you to make the trip, but on your own."

Dickens wondered at the request, and why they should not travel together, but then remembered what Captain Roe had said, that a Ben Hamilton had vouched for Kruge's epiphany, and that Hamilton lived in New Windsor.

"Meet me at the George Washington Inn at seven o'clock," Kruge said. "You'll find the inn readily marked on the way, and everyone knows of it. The inn was headquarters to Washington the last eighteen months of the war, until you people finally quit."

As Kruge spoke, he filled a saddlebag with folders and slipped into his riding boots. Then he gave Dickens a folder. "This will give you a feel for what I am doing." At the door, he turned to Dickens. "See you at the inn?"

Dickens nodded. "Seven o'clock."

"And you'll be needing a place to stay," Kruge said.

"Mr. Micawley has offered me a pallet," Dickens replied.

Kruge narrowed his eyes. "Right, well . . ." He tossed Dickens a set of keys. "Lock up when you leave."

Chapter Twelve

After locking up, Dickens visited the wheelwright shop, finding Micawley at his lathe surrounded by wood chips and sawdust. He told Micawley of Kruge's departure for Newburgh and his agreement to join Kruge at the George Washington Inn for seven o'clock. Micawley allowed the lathe to slow to a stop, and then took a framed parchment from the wall behind his desk. He handed it to Dickens, and Dickens examined it. "This is Washington's signature?"

"Yes."

"And given to your father?"

"For what he did, which is not mentioned in what Washington writes, which is well enough, for it is something to be forgotten. Indeed many Americans do not even know it happened."

"I don't understand," Dickens said.

"After so many years at war, it suddenly comes to a halt. We've got better than seven thousand of your countrymen prisoner, courtesy of Cornwallis at Yorktown, and you British occupy New York City. You no longer want to fight, and we no longer want to be fought. So everyone is waiting for the details of peace, which takes more than a year to frame. As the months drag on, and knowing that we'd won the war, our troops are thinking they ought finally to be paid for the service they've rendered our country. That, of course, is all well and good, except that the Continental Congress has no money, for nobody pays taxes. We've not two pennies to rub together. So the army's bellies and purses are filled with promises only, a recipe for disaster. And that's where Washington comes in . . ." Micawley's eyes suddenly grew moist. "So very much on that man's shoulders, my father would tell me."

Dickens listened, not knowing what to expect.

"It was in March of 1783. That's when my father overhears officers talking, of a letter being circulated about the lack of promised pay and pensions, that perhaps a visit should be paid to congress to settle accounts, an armed visit if necessary. Though a wheelwright at the time, previously my father cared for Washington's horses, so he was able to approach the man, and tell him what was afoot."

"This is incredible," Dickens declared, shaking his head.

"My father said that's when Washington fought his greatest battle—but not with might. He surprises the officers who have assembled in a church to plan their mutinous deed. The church is in Newburgh, north of here, a place called The Temple of Virtue, which you can see for yourself. Anyway, when Washington appears, the officers are shocked to see their commander, and he is not entirely welcomed. In the awkwardness of the moment lay the future of our country, whether for democracy, dictatorship, or some form of monarchy."

Micawley wiped his eyes. "I apologize, Mr. Dickens, it's just . . . to know your father was a part of something so defining . . ." Micawley cleared his throat. "Father said that Washington put on his spectacles and addressed his officers, many who had served the entire war with him, saying not only had he grown gray but almost blind in service to his country. Then, from memory, he delivered what he had penned on parchment and is in a glass case at the inn—the speech that saved the nation. When Washington is done, every man in the room is shamed, many to tears, stricken by the words of their commander, their beloved leader. And that was the end of it."

"Bravo!" Dickens declared. "Truly remarkable, your Washington."

"Who missed seeing the year 1800 by only seventeen days, and it was Washington who bequeathed my father what allowed him to open this shop." Micawley replaced the framed parchment. "You'll enjoy the inn. A lot of history there and in New Windsor."

"Which reminds me . . . do you know of a Mr. Hamilton in New Windsor? He runs a mercantile store."

"Ben Hamilton? Of course, and I wouldn't be surprised that the missus was there today."

At Dickens's request, Micawley wrote out directions to Hamilton's store.

Their attention was drawn to the sound of a hard gallop, ceasing outside the shop.

Micawley raced to the door and swung it open. "James Washington Micawley," Micawley shouted, "this better be the last time I tell you to trot your horse in town! Do you hear me?"

Dickens heard a faint, *yessum*.

"Now you come inside, and let's have your report. Mr. Dickens is here."

The bright-eyed boy, dust covered, appeared in the doorway, face streaked with sweat and bearing a wide toothy grin.

"How did it go, Master James," Dickens asked.

"Delivered your note, sir. To Captain Roe, sir," the boy spoke in short spurts, winded from the ride. "Said to tell you . . . your wife is much better . . . that he is looking after her . . . and not to worry."

Dickens shook the boy's hand vigorously. "You are indeed a most remarkable young man, James, and have done me a great service." He winked at the boy. "I trust you find good use for your wages."

"Oh yes, sir. Thank you, sir. I already know what I want."

"And what is that?" His grandfather asked.

The boy turned to his grandfather. "In Mr. Martin's store, he has a Swiss watch. It's used, but he says it works fine. And, Grandpa, it's silver, and beautiful, and comes with a chain."

Micawley nodded. "I think I know the one, and a wise choice, James. Punctuality is a gentleman's best friend."

The boy flashed the gold coin that Dickens had given him. "I think it is enough, Grandpa."

"I'm sure it is, or Mr. Martin is not a good man of business. Now you get home for chores. And be cleaned up by six when your grandma comes home." As the lad turned on his heels, Micawley called after him, "And use soap!"

"Yes, Grandpa," the boy said, reaching the door, and spinning around, grinning. "Thank you, again, Mr. Dickens. But I would have done it for nothing to ride Grandpa's horse."

Before Dickens could reply, the boy was out the door.

"An exceptional lad, Mr. Micawley. I pray mine grow up as fine."

"James has got his mischief, Mr. Dickens, but thank you. We are blest, the missus and me." Micawley extended his hand. "So you'll be off, and I'll not see you again?"

Taking Micawley's hand, Dickens held onto it. "A minute more, please. There is something I don't understand, which will cost me sleep unless I do. You and Kruge, the best of friends when kids . . . what happened?"

Micawley crossed his arms, and looked at the floor. "His uncle happened—that's what happened. It was just after the dark wood incident, when his mother died. Daniel was still healing. I knew it was no good with his uncle and told him so, that if we didn't spend time together, our friendship, our bond would be gone. At the time, my father had been showing the three of us how to make a wheel, and Eben had wanted to learn, and so he did come by . . . for a while."

"How long?"

"Not long. So soon, he is under his uncle's thumb. I'm sure he resisted as best he could—because he was a tough kid. But his uncle was a mean one, with words and a belt, and a drinking man. One day after school, Kruge tells me he's not to have any friends, not even me, that if it is found out he did, he'll get the licking of his life. I told him I understood, and would not be the cause of such a thing, but that he was to know I would never stop being his friend, and that went for Daniel, too."

"But that didn't happen, did it?" Dickens said.

"Friendship is a back and forth thing, and for us . . ." Micawley let it go. "But more importantly, Mr. Dickens, what you don't know is that Kruge holds the paper on my shop, and has for years."

"A mortgage?" Dickens asked.

"Not the normal mortgage, where if you make payments, your loan is secure. The paper is of his uncle's design, for he is the one I had to deal with. And why I did it, I have no excuse, except that it was a very tough time. My blacksmith shed burnt to the ground, and had to be rebuilt. No way I can sell a wagon wheel without a rim. And there were other debts." Micawley gave an equivocal gesture. "His was the only money available. Anyway, by the paper on the loan, Kruge can take it all—shut me down, anytime he wants. It doesn't matter if I'm current on the loan."

"Hence, the peace offering?"

Micawley nodded.

Chapter Thirteen

Colonel took to the Newburgh road as if he knew it well, and Dickens allowed him his own pace. The rolling landscape, with sheep and other livestock feeding on lush grasses along the way, reminded him of the Cotswolds. At Moodna Creek, Dickens allowed Colonel time to drink. Then Colonels hoofs clopped across the wooden bridge and up the next hill. At the crest, was a sign for New Windsor, and to the right, through gaps in the tree line, Dickens saw the Hudson River. Following Micawley's directions, Dickens found the storefront for Hamilton Mercantile, and a man behind the counter settling a dry goods sale. When the sale was complete and the patron gone, Dickens approached the counter.

"Pardon me, but if you are Ben Hamilton, I know of you through Captain Roe, of the West Point Hotel."

The man behind the counter warmed immediately. "Ah, yes, the good Captain. And what is it you are you in need of?"

"Information only, if you're agreeable; information about the man, Eben Kruge."

"Information," Hamilton said, confused.

"I . . ." Dickens wasn't sure how to begin. "I understand that in the recent past you visited West Point and the hotel, and talked with Roe, that you said, in Kruge, you had witnessed a remarkable change. And I just wanted to confirm that this is so."

Hamilton smiled as he nodded. "In fact, I had just come from Cornwall and meeting with Kruge when I met with Roe. But, I don't understand. What is that to you?"

"I have been with Mr. Kruge most of the day . . . to assess the change you described."

"Do not doubt it, Mister . . . ?"

"Dickens, sir. Charles Dickens." Dickens was relieved when Hamilton did not react to his name.

"A week before I visit Captain Roe, I am in Kruge's office," Hamilton said. "I have by then exhausted every other option to finance a large shipment of fine textiles from France. I know of Kruge's history and his egregious terms, but am prepared to do whatever is necessary, the fabrics being such a bargain, and me with ready buyers. Anyway, he is about to leave his office for an appointment, but with much persistence on my part he allows me to state my need, which I do. He then takes from a drawer a schedule of what he calls his standard fees for services, the interest he would charge on lent funds, the collateral he would require . . . all that sort of thing, all exorbitant. He gives me an appointment for two days later at ten o'clock in the morning. He tells me that if I don't appear, he'll assume I have made other arrangements."

"That sounds like Kruge," Dickens said.

"I, of course, have no other arrangements, and two days later knock on his door at the appointed time, ready to stomach what ever he's serving. But when he opens the door," Hamilton threw up his hands, "I can tell something is different. He's different. No smile, but neither the scowl I witnessed our last meeting. So, I unfold the sheet of terms he has given me, to request the least disadvantageous terms, and he shakes his head, saying he thinks he can do better. And he does. He gives me an interest rate matching the lowest of any of the banks around, gives me a payment schedule that is more than fair, charges me a third of his stated price for preparing and filing the loan papers, and says, if I am agreeable, because he's checked me out, he'll not require any collateral other than the goods I am purchasing. I, of course, agree, and we settle the deal that day." Hamilton shook his head in disbelief. "This was not the man I saw two days earlier. Truly this man's black had turned to white."

Dickens smiled at hearing of the metaphor a second time. "And, if you can remember, when was that, the exact date if possible?"

"Not a problem," Hamilton said, slipping around the counter to his desk. A moment later, he appeared with a document in hand. "The loan is dated March 30, and we settled the deal two days earlier. So that would have been the 28th, the day after Easter."

Departing Hamilton's office, Dickens arrived at the George Washington Inn half an hour later. It was a large fieldstone structure, originally a farmhouse, accompanied by stables, barns, water wells, a large cistern, a smoke house, several chicken coops, and a pigeon house. A long, low split-log structure stood to the side, which Dickens imagined in former days, must have housed troops. In nearby fenced fields was a pasture for horses and grazing lands for cattle and sheep.

Arriving at the inn, Dickens was greeted by a young man in a Continental Army uniform, bearing a musket with fixed bayonet. The man wore a tri-cornered hat, white linen shirt and vest, dark blue woolen topcoat with brass buttons, crossed white belts and cartridge box, white cotton breeches, stockings, and buckled leather shoes. He saluted Dickens with his musket and then exclaimed in a louder than necessary voice, "Welcome to the George Washington Inn, sir, war-time home of the first president and first lady of the United States of America. I hope you will enjoy your visit, sir."

Dickens nodded, approvingly.

"Shall I graze your horse, sir?'

"Yes, and an apple, too, if you can manage it."

"I'm sure I can, sir." The young man's stoic face suddenly betrayed a smile. "Pardon, sir, but from your accent I take you as a former enemy?"

Dickens returned an affecting smile. "But now a staunch ally."

"Yes, sir, and thank you, sir. Will you be long, sir?"

"I'm early for a seven o'clock supper, if you can gauge by that."

"Very good, sir." The man motioned with his head to the inn. "There is much to entertain you inside."

Dickens, carrying the folder, entered a foyer through a door rigged with a bell, the ringing of which produced a lady, also in period costume.

"You're a bit early for supper, sir," the lady announced in a cheery voice, "but the bar is open and it looks down upon the valley and river." The woman curtsied. "And my name is Molly."

"You are too kind, Molly," Dickens replied. "I mean to take a look at some of what is about this place, and then will report directly to the bar."

The woman loosed a light titter, "I love you British."

The foyer boasted walls that could not be seen for all that hung upon them, mostly oil paintings and artfully colored etchings of landscapes, portraits, and men in uniform, all complimented by a variety of precisely drawn maps. Dickens invested himself in the whole, discerning from it, a history inglorious to the motherland. His meanderings led to a hall, which boasted more articles of history; a wall display of swords, sabers, pistols, and muskets; and a large glass case bearing a brass plate inscribed *General George Washington, Commander in Chief, Continental Army, United States of America*, the case enclosing a regal uniform and saber. Also, in the case were several letters written by Washington, but not the speech that Micawley had mentioned.

In the bar, Dickens observed four men at a table by a window that overlooked the river, and from the sound and appearance of the men and their table, Dickens judged them to be having a high time despite the early hour. Hardly had he taken a seat at the bar, when the bartender, a round, red-faced, well-bearded man asked for his order. As quickly as Dickens gave the order, his drink was placed on the bar with a bowl of walnuts. Dickens retrieved a cigar from his vest pocket, and leaned in to the match offered by the bartender.

"You're looking mighty dapper, sir," the bartender said, extending his hand. "Name's Peter Hawkins."

Dickens took Hawkins's hand. "So this is your first president's headquarters."

"At the time, running the Army, and the war won. Though it was a testy time for him, what with the troops restless, and for good reason."

"Over what?" Dickens asked, already knowing the answer.

"Another round of ale, Peter," one of the men at the table shouted. The man got up and approached the bar. Dickens recognized him as the tall man who had been Kruge's second visitor that morning. Dickens made a point of nodding, and the man not only nodded back, but smiled, and asked, "What are you drinking, sir?"

"Cider," Dickens replied.

"Only cider?" the man said. "Peter, bring my friend another cider."

When the man rejoined his three friends and the ales were served, his friends toasted him with "For He's a Jolly Good Fellow." A short time later, they arose as one and departed, the tall man palming something into the bartender's hand that brought forth a grin and an expression of heart-felt thanks.

Hawkins turned to Dickens. "A fine fellow, that Martin."

"I should say so," Dickens said. "That he would buy a drink for me, a stranger, and an Englishman to boot, is a stretch."

The bartender smiled. "None better, and that's a fact."

"Celebrating something, is he?"

"He's come into good news, sir. And long deserved, I should say, so ill-used he was by a scoundrel and most odious man in Cornwall. Tells me he has regained control of his logging company, that he can afford to be generous again."

Dickens was about to press the point, but reconsidered. "About General Washington, you were saying . . . an issue?"

"Lord, not just an issue, but one that could have undone the country. It's almost legend around these parts."

Dickens returned a blank look, and allowed Hawkins to relate an only slightly different version of the story told by Micawley, but containing no mention of Washington's informant.

"And a copy of his speech is penned on the parchment in that glass case there." Hawkins pointed to a display case on the east wall, between windows that overlooked the Hudson. "The speech that saved our freedoms." Hawkins said with pride. "So, another cider?"

"No. But I'll take a look at the speech." Dickens ambled over to the glass case and read twice what Washington had written, and marveled at the man's capacity for persuasion. He then sat at the table vacated by the four gentlemen, and opened the folder from Kruge, thumbing through forty or so account ledgers. As he did, the front door opened so often, that it produced an almost continuous ringing of the bell, and Dickens wondered if there would be a table left for he and Kruge. When Dickens came to the ledger for Martin, he reviewed in detail the entries, which included a listing of owners and their percentage interests in the company each time a material change in ownership occurred. Up until the latest entry, Kruge owned fifty-one percent of the company, but the latest entry showed him having no interest in the company, and Martin's interest increased by fifty-one percent.

The bell rung again, and Dickens glanced once more at the door, and saw Kruge bearing a most curious expression.

Chapter Fourteen

Kruge gestured to Dickens, and in the dining room they were given a table that had just turned. But as quickly as they sat down, a middle-aged man in a linen blouse, cotton trousers, and riding boots approached them.

"Mr. Kruge, sir," the man said, a broad-brimmed hat in his hand, "I've been sent to beg a moment of your time? I know it's not convenient."

"Indeed," Kruge said tersely, "it is most inconvenient."

"Sir, it is important. I would not have come, otherwise. And you will want to know what I have to say . . . and give you."

Kruge turned to Dickens, who nodded his assent. "Very well. Mr. Dickens, I recommend that you order the evening special for both of us, and whatever you'd like to drink. The specials are excellent and quickly served, and come with the house wine." Kruge followed the man out of the dining room.

Fifteen minutes later Kruge reappeared, his countenance grave.

"Is everything in order, Mr. Kruge?" Dickens asked.

Kruge said nothing, and after a few sips of wine seemed to regain himself. After applying cutlery to roasted duck, yams, and green beans, Kruge spoke, "I am puzzled about the story in your Bible, about the rich man and Lazarus—not the one raised from the dead—but the beggar at the rich man's gate."

"The parable."

"I suppose." Kruge bore a look of earnestness. "When the beggar dies, angels take him to heaven, but when the rich man dies . . . he goes . . . the other direction. There is no explanation that the rich man was bad or that the beggar was good. Where is the justice in that, sir?"

"Perhaps," Dickens said, shaking his head, "you are too much the lawyer. You must understand that the Bible is for all humankind, young and old. Try to see the message through the lens of a child, that those who live for themselves, which often are the rich that have no sense of needing faith, have placed their hearts in possessions and the things of this world. While those who are poor, abandoned, and destitute have placed their faith in God and the promise of heaven."

"But rich people can do good, can they not?"

"They can, and do, but some who do good, do so for its own reward, and not to God's glory."

"So confusing," Kruge said, rubbing his temples. "Regardless, Mr. Dickens, I mean to tell you a number of things before we return to Cornwall . . . to prepare you."

"And I am obliged to know it. But, if I may, a question first?"

"What is it?"

"The lady in black, your third visitor?"

"The widow Watson," Kruge replied.

"Leaving your office, she asked if I had been set up as she had been, perceiving me to be, I suppose, one of your clients."

Kruge stopped, mid bite, his expression having turned anxious. "What did she tell you?"

"Nothing. She didn't tell me anything. She said she could no more tell me, than I could tell her."

Kruge seemed to breathe more easily. "Nothing else?"

"Only that we would find out soon enough."

"Um . . . indeed," Kruge said in a resigned tone.

Dickens retrieved a sheet from the folder. "Reviewing the ledger for Mrs. Watson, it appears her husband borrowed a large sum from you before he died, some ten thousand dollars, but the last entry, made this morning, shows the debt forgiven."

"His investment was in a furring company. We advanced the funds, knowing that the venture would be unsuccessful, given the company's management and its propensity to squander capital. In our loan contract, we required pledge of Watson's significant land holdings along the Hudson, north of Newburgh, in the event the venture soured, which it did in less than two years. Watson, a much overweight man, and too old and enfeebled to be riding, took a fall from a horse soon after, and died from his injuries. That was when we called on the loan and interest outstanding. Mrs. Watson had no liquid assets, so we exercised our contractual right to take the pledged land holdings. It was very difficult on the lady, but she is a proud woman, and has managed to keep her home, with a stipend for expenses."

"The value of the land?"

"Easily twenty to twenty-five thousand dollars, with newly constructed dock facilities."

"And you deeded it back to her?"

"I did."

"But why the secrecy, sir?" Dickens shrugged. "It is clear you are settling debts, making amends with those in your web."

Kruge did not answer.

"In the same vain, sir," Dickens continued, "upon my arrival here at the inn, I encountered your second visitor this morning, the tall man. This morning, when I passed him at your door, he was anxious and ignored me completely. This afternoon, when he is with three others in the bar, he is most engaging and in a merry mood, indeed."

Kruge's eyes narrowed. "What did the man say?"

"A greeting, only. But the bartender, who seems to know him well, said that he had come into good news, that he had regained what was lost and wanted to celebrate."

"Therein lies what keeps me awake at night, Mr. Dickens. The uncertainty of promise."

"I miss your meaning, sir," Dickens said.

"Human nature, sir, our bent to act contrary. Take my first visitor this morning, Gerald Small."

Dickens smiled at the name, remembering the short man who could not have been more than thirty.

"He grows up in Cornwall to age sixteen with a father and no mother. In the last of those years, he falls in with some bad sorts suspected of petty crimes, but never caught. He has a row with his father, who thinks the worst of him, and runs off to Baltimore to prove himself. About two years ago, the father dies, leaving a small farm to the estranged son. The boy, now a man, returns, by all appearances, a changed man. But then, one day, he is arrested by the sheriff for poaching game and stealing goods from the Military Academy, the most significant being a yoke of oxen. Another man says there is proof of Small's guilt at his farm. The sheriff searches the farm, and finds one of the oxen, with a federal brand, in an old hay shed, the beast nearly down with disease. Small claims his innocence, that he knows nothing of it."

"But what is that to you?"

"He needs an attorney, and I knew his father in my better days. I agreed to represent him, but in return required, if I got him off, that he pay me ten percent of his earnings."

"For how long?"

"For life, which he agreed to, and has done."

"So you proved him innocent?"

"Never got to court. The snitch was one of Small's old friends, himself in and out of jail since Small left Cornwall. I paid a visit to the snitch's place and found the other ox in a small barn; the yoke in the corner of the barn had *US Army* burned into the wood; wool blankets and the like nearby."

"Was this not a good thing you did?" Dickens said.

"I spend a few hours on Small's behalf, and in return subject him to a life of obligation? Hardly fair—at least to my current mind."

Dickens nodded.

"Anyway, as you saw, he was quaking when he entered my office, no doubt, suspecting a demand from me. But when I forgive his obligation, make it clear he owes me nothing, his nature changes completely, not for the bad, mind you, for he is entirely grateful, but what is to happen? A renewed self esteem, what will it bring? Will he meet his end of the bargain?"

"You've lost me, sir."

Kruge pushed his plate aside. "I am under an obligation that I fear will undo me, that is beyond my control."

"Sir?"

Kruge drained his wine glass. As he did, Dickens retrieved two cigars, handing one to Kruge, and lighting them both.

"On the day of my uncle's death," Kruge said, "I was confronted by what you will see tonight, by what you will not believe, until you do."

Dickens laughed lightly. "You make me think I'm to see a ghost."

Kruge blew a smoke ring, and answered, unblinking. "Exactly."

"Pardon?"

"A specter."

Dickens cocked his head. "You are joking?"

Kruge shook his head.

"I'm to see a ghost?" Dickens said.

Kruge nodded, exhaling a thin stream of smoke.

"You can't be serious."

"Or a spirit, a phantom, a ghoul . . . your choice. But that is not the point, for who or what he is, as I say, you will see soon enough."

Kruge's pronouncement and Kruge's bony finger pointed at Dickens's nose had its desired effect.

"Though," Kruge continued, "to my mind, he is more an angel, and has sort of . . . taken me under his wing. Though, in truth, I'm not even sure he is a him."

"And it is this specter-angel that has wrought your change?"

"I have been given very specific instructions."

Kruge refilled his wine glass. "When he first visited me, it was the evening of the burial. My uncle, dead just the day before, it was a challenge to get him in the ground so soon, and the grave digger and I had quite a discussion getting it done on Christmas Day, him protesting the rush on account of the day. Though, you could not convince me he was of a mind to enjoy anything about Christmas."

Kruge flicked the ashes of his cigar on the plank floor.

"Anyway, I offer him a most generous gratuity to get the thing done, which he does, but only after chiseling the first foot of frozen earth and digging the smoking dirt below in as breezy a cold as might come off the Hudson. And it is nigh nightfall when the pine box containing my uncle is in the ground, me helping with the ropes. I am surprised, then, by the appearance of the reverend who says a few words over the miserable wretch, me perceiving much double meaning in all of them."

Kruge sipped his wine. "Then the reverend is gone, and it is just me and the gravedigger. Before filling the hole, he has his hand out, says he won't fill the hole until he is paid in full. I oblige him his due, but after filling the hole only halfway, he tells me he'll finish in the morning, that his hands are frozen, and that he will not be denied a toast to the day and the season." Kruge turned to Dickens. "So then it is only me in the cemetery, with no lamp or lantern."

"And I suppose that's when you first saw the specter?" Dickens said.

"Heard, only, it being overcast, too dark to see anything. But the sound was enough to fright my bones. A man's voice, it was, and as near to me as this glass of wine." Kruge took another sip.

"A voice then." Dickens granted.

"He says, the man down there is going to hell, do you wish to join him?"

"The angel speaks to you this way?"

"Exactly so," Kruge replied. "Like you and me having a conversation. Mock me now, Mr. Dickens, but you will hear and see for yourself." Kruge sat back in his chair, allowing the pronouncement effect. "To his question, whether I'd wished to join my uncle, he added, even before I could answer, that if I did, then I would see him no more. But if I did not, he would come again." Kruge looked hard at Dickens. "Mr. Dickens, I have no desire to join my uncle. So much so, if he were in heaven, I should desire hell. And so I tell the angel, who then commands me to do something, and then is gone."

"Do what?"

"Beware and be ready," is all he said. Nothing more, except that I should know he was privy to all that I did, that he would be watching."

"And that was Christmas Day?"

Kruge nodded.

"So . . . he comes back?" Dickens asked.

Kruge nodded again. "But not for three months, not until the evening of March 27."

"You are that sure of it?"

"It was your resurrection day, what you call, Easter."

"You were in church?"

"Me? I should think not. But it was the day when the gravedigger knocks on my door. He tells me something, grinning as he does, and then leaves me to deal with it."

"Pray tell," Dickens insisted.

"A gravestone was delivered and placed in the cemetery. The gravedigger said my name was on it." Kruge took another sip of wine. "I, of course, did not believe him, but wanted to see for myself, and it was a busy day at the church. So I waited until after dark to enter the cemetery with a lamp. I find the gravestone, and it is next to my uncle's, and it indeed bears my name.

Kruge hesitated. "I am in front of the gravestone, staring at my name, when I hear the voice, the same voice I heard Christmas night, calling my name. I turn, and in the light of the lamp there is a figure, a human form, half again as big as me, but opaque, dressed in white, or bathed in light—I am never quite sure. And he is not in a good mood."

Dickens refilled his empty wine glass from the carafe.

"He tells me I have changed little, that my time is limited, and that without a changed heart and actions to prove it, I will reap no better than my uncle. I protest, but to no avail." Kruge's eyes grew large. "It is then that he tells me to look at the stone."

"Your stone?"

"No, sir. My uncle's stone."

"I don't understand"

"You will. Just a few hours more."

Kruge shook his head. "I look at the stone. What I see is not possible, and I tremble before Gabriel."

"Gabriel?"

"I've come to call him that, though not to his face."

"The stone . . . ?" Dickens pressed.

"Gabriel says I am to have one more chance. And I tell him I can do better, and will, but must know what I am to do. I beg him to tell me."

"And . . . ?"

"He says I am to believe in the one who sent him, understand the wrong I have done, beg for forgiveness, and undo as much of the wrong as I can."

"And the Bible?" Dickens asked.

"That was Micawley's idea, that if I was to believe in God, I should know something about him."

"Then Micawley is aware?"

"Not of Gabriel. Only of me . . . wanting to know about God."

"And what of Micawley? What is it between the two of you?"

"That, sir, is our business," Kruge answered, almost apologetically.

"As you wish," Dickens said, "So, your visitors, this folder . . . for more than two months you've been making amends?"

"Yes, though many of the amends I would make, for myself or as party to my uncle's work, I cannot . . ." Kruge's voice held genuine remorse. "It is too late. And now, almost nightly, I go to the cemetery to see Gabriel. Always at midnight, for he says, I am to come only at midnight."

"Your angel, Gabriel?"

"Yes, and each time I see him, I am judged."

"Judged?"

"On what I've done. Which might seem straightforward. But, I assure you, is not, for there is a caveat."

"How so?"

"None other than the person I have wronged is to know that I am the source of their recompense. I am to beg their forgiveness, and their restitution is to be anonymous."

"But how do you manage that?"

"Not very well, I think. Though, you give me encouragement." Kruge sipped his wine. "With each party," Kruge corrected himself, "with each person I have wronged, I have drawn up a contract to render, in case the other party does not comply, the restitution null and void, with a binding obligation that whatever has been dispersed be returned to me, and re-invoking whatever the terms of the original obligation."

"Um. Very . . . neat and legal."

"Judge me not, sir. How else am I to accomplish what my very life depends upon?"

"And have any been compromised?"

"No. Not as yet. Not to my knowledge."

"So the rest of the world knows nothing of your epiphany?"

"Only, I suppose, that in business, I am not the man I was."

"And where do you stand?"

"I'm very nearly done, but also very nearly out of money."

"Does that concern you . . . the money . . . giving it away . . . not having it."

"It was all I lived for . . . but no longer."

Chapter Fifteen

Dickens and Kruge rode in the buggy back to Cornwall, with Kruge's horse tethered to the boot of the buggy. It was time enough for Kruge to summarize more misdealings, and consequent efforts and expenses to right wrongs, lamenting the tentacled trails of misery he had wrought, his remorse touching Dickens's heart.

As Colonel crossed the bridge over Moodna Creek, Dickens turned to Kruge. "Sir, I've heard from Mr. Micawley about the dark wood, that you, he, and another boy found it, and a little about what happened. But he declined to give me details."

Kruge let the statement hang in the air before answering. "The third boy was Daniel Rourke."

Dickens nodded.

"I still dream of it," Kruge said, "and it is not a pleasant dream."

"Can you talk about it?" Dickens asked.

"What did Jedidiah tell you?" Kruge asked.

"Only that you found the wood, that you were in it, and that there was a sound or music that made you run."

"As fast as we could. But what of Daniel?"

"Only that he was with you, and, I'm to believe . . . was hurt?"

"Aye," Kruge said. "Such an unpleasant business, and us so innocent. We were in the dark wood maybe half an hour . . . dark, yes, but we felt no dread. No evidence of kidnappings . . . Micawley told you of the missing girls?"

Dickens nodded.

"Anyway, we are eating and joking, and can't wait to get back and show proof of our being there, when there was, like you say, this sound, like singing . . . quiet at first. We had heard about the women of the Lenape tribe, that they would sing or chant to the spirit world. We all look at each other, wondering what to do. And then it gets louder, and, to my mind, closer, something I could almost feel. Micawley was first on his feet and was away. Daniel and I followed on his heels, me a pace ahead of Daniel, so I didn't see it."

"See what?" Dickens asked.

"We are running as fast as legs can carry, between trees the diameter of this buggy. The forest floor is pine needles, hiding roots and everything else. We are sprinting downhill, the music following us, when Daniel trips. I hear him hit the ground, and I hear him scream." Kruge hesitated. "You want to hear this?"

"I must."

"I look behind, and Daniel is face down in the pine needles."

Dickens felt his skin crawl.

"So close, we are. The light at the edge of the wood is so close. I wanted to keep running. The sound was too much, pounding my ears, so loud now." Kruge lowered his head. "I went back for him."

Dickens's heart raced.

"When I got to him, he was sobbing. I rolled him over." Kruge turned to Dickens. "Mr. Dickens, half of Daniel's face is gone."

Dickens grimaced.

"His father's skinning knife . . . razor sharp," Kruge was nearly incoherent in his speech. "Before the singing . . . cutting an apple . . . for all of us . . . must have run with it . . . don't know . . ." Kruge appeared to hyperventilate. "The right side of his face is laid open from his eye to his chin . . . blood everywhere . . . I can see the white of his cheek bone and jaw."

Dickens shuddered.

Kruge drew a flask from his waistcoat and took a pull. "Suddenly, there is silence, the music is gone. Daniel . . . he asks if it is bad . . . is he okay? I lie . . . I say he's fine. He says . . . he can't feel anything . . . asks me if I found his knife." Kruge had to clear his throat. "Then the music returns. It is upon us, pine needles start flying around us. I roll his skin back, and tie it down best I can to the bone with my kerchief. I tell him to hold it down, not let go. All the time, he's pleading . . . not to leave him. I get him to his feet."

Kruge pulled on the flask again. "The edge of the wood can't be thirty feet away, and I think it is too late. But that's when the music stops and the streaks of light appear, swirling everywhere, coming together around Daniel's head. He screams again, or at least I think he's screaming. I look at him and the streaks of light around his head are now one solid, brilliant mass. So bright, I can't look at it. And then . . ."

"What?" Dickens demanded.

"The light is gone. It is dark again . . . except for the light at the edge of the wood. Daniel is stone still on the ground, and I think he is dead. All is silent, but then Daniel starts to move. He sits up, as if from a nap, still clutching his face. He shakes his head. My kerchief is missing. I kneel next to him, and pry his fingers from his face. Mr. Dickens, there is no bleeding, the blood on his face is gone, and he says there is no pain. The laceration is seared to a scar, a long, jagged scar . . . as it is to this day."

Kruge took another pull on his flask. "Tell me about justice, Mr. Dickens. Tell me why such a thing could happen. Minutes before, Daniel is handsome, the most popular boy in our school. Every girl's eye is upon him. And I am jealous as hell. But in an instant, he is hideous. I can barely look at him."

Kruge took yet another pull on the flask.

"Is Daniel a carpenter?" Dickens asked, his eyes on Colonel.

Kruge nearly dropped his flask. "How did you know?"

"Doesn't matter," Dickens said. "But that you were faithful to him, that you went back, that's what matters." Dickens shook his head. "Upon my soul, Mr. Kruge from what you've said, I swear I would have outrun Jedidiah, and, to be honest, I'm not sure I could have gone back for Daniel."

Kruge seemed not to hear. "That day ended our innocence, none of us the same after. We had been blood brothers, the three of us doing everything together for almost two years." Kruge turned to Dickens. "Daniel is one of the two people in Cornwall I have yet to right. And I have wronged him most grievously."

The buggy jolted through a rut.

"Though, I suppose it wasn't me, at least not directly, and I could not prevent it, which is what I tried to tell Daniel. But it was more than twenty years ago. Daniel was living with his mother, taking care of her. His father, a failing entrepreneur, died nine years earlier, leaving a big house, but little money. Daniel never married . . . the scar and all. Unknown to me, my uncle holds the mortgage on his mother's house. When she misses a third payment, my uncle pounces on her, giving her thirty days to vacate."

Kruge took another pull on the flask. "My appeals had no effect. He killed her as sure as with a gun. In her late sixties, maybe seventies, she doesn't survive the winter, and Daniel is beyond rage, and won't have anything to do with me, and for twenty years he's avoided me. He lives a hermit's life in a one-room tenement, and works only to pay bills. He could have done so much better. The fact is, Daniel is the finest carpenter in the Highlands . . . next to Micawley."

"You never speak?" Dickens asked.

"When I see him, I can't face him. I'm too ashamed. You see . . . months after the foreclosure, I moved into his mother's house."

Chapter Sixteen

Dickens dropped Kruge and his horse at Kruge's office, and returned to the livery to bed Colonel for the night, giving the livery groom notice of his departure early the next morning. As he was leaving, Dickens encountered the Presbyterian Church sexton.

"So you've had a nice visit with Mr. Kruge?" the sexton said, tongue-in-cheek

Wanting information from the man, Dickens smiled. "Might I ask you a question?"

"It's a free country, sir. You can do anything you like."

"Yes," Dickens said lightly. "This past Easter, do you recall mentioning to Kruge something about a gravestone?"

The question elicited a broad grin. "I did, and it was more than my pleasure to do so."

"The news of his gravestone being delivered?"

"That was part of it."

"There was more?"

The sexton gave Dickens a look. "He didn't tell you? But then I suppose, how could he? For there is no explanation for it, and the likes of you would have thought him off his spot, if you know what I mean."

"No, I don't know what you mean," Dickens said.

"This morning, I told you I keep the place neat and tidy . . . everything and everyone in their place?"

"Yes."

"Well. On Easter Day, when Kruge's stone is delivered, I watch it being set, and while I'm there, watching, I see nearby something amiss. Something very strange." From the livery, a voice called out to the sexton." Responding to the summons, the sexton repeated over his shoulder, "Something very strange, indeed."

When Dickens rejoined Kruge, it was dark, and two whale oil lamps lit the front portion of the office. On Kruge's desk was a third, smaller lamp, which was unlit. After seating himself, Dickens spoke, "Sir, I presume what will happen tonight takes place at the Presbyterian Church cemetery. Am I right?"

Kruge was about to speak, but hesitated.

"Sir, why would you leave me ignorant of what will happen?" Dickens said, his irritation evident.

"Mr. Dickens, please. You must know I would not intentionally hide anything from you . . . not now, and, of course, you already know of Gabriel. And I want you to know it all, for it is my hope that your knowing it will benefit me. But what limitations our language has. I am at a loss as to how I can describe what you will experience. But, yes, our destination is the cemetery. Now, can you be patient?"

"As you wish," Dickens said, reluctantly.

"But I can offer you a little courage," Kruge said, attempting a smile. "You will need it, and I could use it."

As Kruge went to a cabinet, Dickens mused aloud, "I must say, sir, the day is more than living up to its billing, perhaps the most unusual day of my life—real or imagined—and what will happen at midnight is all but killing my cat."

Kruge smiled thinly, as he returned with a bottle and two shot glasses, topping off each glass.

With firmness of purpose, Kruge raised his glass, "To the only man who will ever know my secret."

After clinking, Dickens took a sip and smiled. "Kentucky?"

Kruge gave him a look. "You know us that well?"

Both men drained their glasses, and Kruge charged them a second time, emptying the bottle, Dickens wondering at how much alcohol the attorney had already imbibed.

Content to sip the second glass, Dickens asked, "Do you live alone, sir?"

"A housekeeper . . . the woman who served our midday meal . . . who, no doubt, thinks me crazy."

"How's that?"

"After Easter, I tripled her salary and ran her off for a week of vacation, for which I paid."

Dickens smiled again. "Good on you, sir."

The evening passed with nothing of note, except that Kruge grew self-absorbed and visibly agitated, several times getting up and pacing the room.

At eleven-fifteen, Kruge lit the smaller lamp, fitted the glass cover in place, and rose to his feet.

"Let me show you something, Mr. Dickens," Kruge said, leading Dickens to the rear of the office, to the trunk that Dickens had seen Kruge visit twice that morning. "Please, open the chest. It is not locked."

Dickens did as he was asked, and was surprised by what he saw.

"What do you see?"

"I thought there would be more . . . but only what you showed me earlier—the boat, candlestick, and lockbox."

"Look closer . . . please."

Dickens did, and saw at the bottom of the chest a small envelope, yellowed with age. He removed it, and found it brittle to the touch, and inside a lock of fine blond hair. He turned to Kruge, whose face was unreadable. "Your Abigail?"

"Such defines my life," Kruge replied. "Now we must be off."

Entering the night, Dickens found the air warm and sultry, the sky admitting only a few stars and a quarter moon. Kruge suggested that he leave his coat in Micawley's shop, which Dickens did. Emerging from the shop, Dickens followed close on Kruge's heels, Kruge moving resolutely down Main Street, the thoroughfare illumined only at intersections by gas lampposts. As they approached the Cornwall Presbyterian Church, Kruge opened the cemetery gate.

Inside the gate, only the quarter moon marked the dark night sky. Kruge finally broke silence, "Before we go into the sanctuary and await midnight, you must see something, Mr. Dickens." He held the lamp high, and proceeded down the center lane of the cemetery, the packed gravel surface upon which tenants arrived by wagon. The lane divided the roughly square cemetery in half. As they advanced, the light from Kruge's lamp illuminated rectangular footprints of sunken earth, and grave markers of varied design and construction, some unreadable for age or growth of algae. Fresh flowers adorned two of the tombstones, and no wilted flowers were to be seen. Near the far end of the cemetery, Kruge stopped. "Follow me." He turned left and proceeded gingerly along the foot of five grave plots to a sixth plot, where not much grass had taken root. He raised his lamp above the gravestone at the head of the plot. "What do you read, Mr. Dickens?"

Dickens read the stone, "*Hans Gerber Roth . . . Born November 3, 1765 . . . Died December 24, 1841 . . . Son of the Fallen Star.*" Dickens turned to Kruge. "Your uncle?"

Kruge nodded.

Dickens repeated the last line, "*Son of the Fallen Star* . . . curious . . . and do you understand its meaning?"

"At first, no," Kruge replied, "but then I asked Micawley, and he explained it, that the Fallen Star is Lucifer . . . Satan himself." Kruge pointed to the marker again. "But look carefully at the stone, at the face and the inscription." Kruge held the lamp closer for Dickens. "Do you see anything unusual?"

Dickens did as requested, finding the engraving well done and the letters easy to read. Wondering at Kruge's question, he answered, "I should like mine crafted as well."

"Indeed, excellent workmanship, even flawless."

"I don't understand."

"Sir, until Easter, the last line read, *A Good Man of Business*. That is what my uncle directed be etched in the marble of that stone, and finely done it was. But come Easter Day, that line is as you read. Explain that to me! How does stone repair itself and be re-cut, with no evidence of its happening?"

Dickens considered, arriving at what he thought was the obvious answer. "The stone is a new one, sir, replacing the old one when yours was placed. Someone playing a trick on you, I should think."

"Nay, sir. I should not be that much a fool. Look at the right corner of the stone." Kruge put his finger upon it. "See the chip here? In the stonecutter's haste to set the stone last Christmas, it fell from the wagon and was damaged, but only here at the corner. It is the same chip, the same stone. I stake my life on it."

Dickens said nothing.

"Now," Kruge declared, swinging the lamp to the next gravestone. "What do you read here, sir?"

Dickens examined the adjacent stone, judging it to be the same marble, and likely the same quarry, though of a lighter shade. "The stone, sir, bears what I suppose is your full name, *Eben Andrew Kruge*. And the lettering is a bit different than what is on your uncle's stone. Otherwise, the stone is smooth, polished, and blank."

"Exactly! The same marble, but less weathered," Kruge said, as though proving his point.

"But why this stone for you . . . and why Easter?"

"Purchased by my uncle, the deal being better if he buys two plots and two stones. I find out only later, after he's dead. He paid more than half the invoice out of funds escrowed to my account, and jotted justification in the payments ledger that my stone was larger and had fewer flaws." Kruge paused. "As to why, Easter . . . I've never thought about it."

Dickens gestured at the two stones. "Then, you are to be neighbors."

"Nay, sir," Kruge snapped, sharply. "I have asked for a different plot."

Chapter Seventeen

Inside the sanctuary, Kruge sat on the front pew, near the side door to the cemetery, the oil lamp on the floor in front of him. Dickens sat beside him, Kruge staring fixedly at the cased window directly beneath the eve of the shadowed wall. Through the window, ambient light from the partial moon cast a feint shadow on the aisle in front of the wooden cross.

Kruge broke silence, his eye on the lamp. "I want so to change, Mr. Dickens, and I must, but think that I am too set in my ways, in all that forms my being. The muscles of my face have forgotten how to smile. I embarrass myself in a mirror, attempting to do so. What I see is comical, or pitiful, but not the face of gladness. This morning, the few times I attempted to laugh, your response affirmed it. You found me offensive."

"So many years a certain way, you must give it time. Real change takes time."

"How much time, Mr. Dickens? Gabriel speaks to me of joy, and I so want to know it and spread it. But how am I to spread what I do not understand?"

"Again, sir, patience."

For a moment, neither spoke, until Kruge said, "Earlier you questioned my belief in miracles."

"I believe it was the other way around, sir," Dickens said lightly, not wanting to be argumentative.

"No matter. Soon you will witness what you came for, and if you do not believe it to be a miracle, at the very least you'll find it a sublime piece of the unnatural."

"Bravo on you, Mr. Kruge," Dickens replied. "Now there's a riddle."

Kruge protested weakly, "Not meant to be."

It was then, in the flickering light of the lamp, that the course of gradual change in Kruge's appearance manifested itself fully to Dickens. The man was entirely undone, and what struck Dickens with stark reality was that whatever had undone Kruge was about to make itself known to him.

During the final minutes leading up to midnight, Dickens found himself continually shifting his gaze from Kruge, to the window, to the cross, to the wall clock, to the side door, and back to Kruge.

When the hour hand reached twelve and the minute hand was but a stroke behind, Dickens found himself unable to keep his tongue. "Mr. Kruge, sir, I do not know whether to be your second in an encounter with the unknown or flee for my life. You have all my senses at lock-kneed attention, waiting for what . . . I have no idea. And I am trembling all over!"

But Kruge said nothing. Not until the minute hand married the hour, at which time a curiously strong wind blew up and buffeted the sanctuary windows. In the instant, Kruge turned to the door, "I am coming!"

Dickens jumped to his feet, his heart pounding. "Mr. Kruge?"

Kruge turned. "Let me handle this, sir." His eyes were as round as the largest of marbles. A great gust of wind threatened to drive in the wall facing the cemetery. "Say nothing, unless he addresses you directly! Otherwise, you are to say nothing. Are we clear!"

Dickens nodded, shrinking back from the face before him, contorted, ashen gray, lips drawn back from uneven teeth, and eyes bloodshot and piercing. This was not the man he had met fifteen hours earlier. This was not the man who would have brooked no ill from anyone. This was a man possessed by fear.

Chapter Eighteen

Outside, Dickens found the night charged with an unnatural energy. Save for the quarter moon, the sky was coal black. Wind whistled through the trees and rattled the church shutters. A sudden gust nearly doused the oil lamp. But Kruge pressed forward, with Dickens at his heels. The first graves in the cemetery rose up to meet them. The musty smell of fresh turned earth was thick in the air.

After a dozen steps, Kruge cocked his head, "He's here, Mr. Dickens. And it is for this you have come."

Presently, they reached the grave plot intended for Kruge. For a long moment, Kruge stared at the gravestone with a look of dread, leaning forward for a closer look and running his fingers across its face. Then, with squinting eyes, he searched the entire cemetery, Dickens following his lead.

"I know you are here!" Kruge shouted. "My friend. Show yourself." The pitch of Kruge's voice chilled Dickens.

"Come out, you . . . ." Kruge suddenly made a sucking sound and shrank back, nearly knocking Dickens off his feet. Kruge waved a boney finger at the gravestone. "Unfair, sir, hiding behind the grave marker, that you can even do so, being so much larger . . . how do you do that?"

Dickens followed Kruge's gaze, but saw nothing.

A moment later, Kruge spoke again, "Him, sir? He is a Mr. Dickens, a gentleman from England."

But in the direction of Kruge's gaze, Dickens saw no one and heard nothing.

"I have," Kruge spoke a third time, with an air of pride. "Three today, and tomorrow, two more, I should think."

Dickens moved to the side of the gravestone, but still saw no one, neither behind the gravestone nor anywhere else within the light of the lamp.

For the next several moments, Kruge carried on what Dickens perceived to be a conversation with himself, his voice at times rising, at times falling, and at times ceasing, as if to listen. At one point, Kruge exclaimed, "But I *have* done my part!" Though in the next instant begging pardon in a most contrite voice as though having been reprimanded. Dickens walked a complete circle around Kruge and the gravestone, and started a second circle. When in Kruge's line of sight, he waved his hands, shouting, "Mr. Kruge, do you see me, sir?"

But so engaged was Kruge, he gave no answer or evidence of notice.

Returning to Kruge's side, Dickens found him pleading, "Please, sir, I'd rather not. It is too much for me." But in the next instant, Kruge nodded submissively. "I understand, sir, but be a comfort, my friend, and I believe you to be my friend. Do not say you are not." Kruge placed the lamp on top of the gravestone, averting his eyes from the gravestone."

Kruge suddenly turned to Dickens, with feral eyes and a finger pointing at the gravestone. "Read, sir, what do you see on my gravestone!"

Dickens shrank back at first, but then stooped before the stone. He inspected it in the light of the lamp. He glanced back at Kruge, whose eyes were still averted from the stone. Dickens ran his hand across the grave marker, not knowing what to say, and so saying nothing.

Kruge glared at Dickens, shouting angrily, "You won't tell me, will you? Then, so be it. Move aside, man!"

Dickens did so, shaken by the whole, and Kruge took hold of the lamp. As he lowered the lamp, he made eye contact with the stone. For a long moment he stood still and silent before the stone, sweeping his fingers across its face, his eyes moving across and down the stone.

Dickens heard the rising sound of a low, guttural moan, its intensity growing to a cry of utter anguish, suddenly masked by a blinding flash and peal of thunder, and the toppling of an elm tree upon a corner of the cemetery.

"Mr. Kruge, sir," Dickens shouted. "Are you well?"

Kruge turned to Dickens, the expression on his face sending an icy chill down the writer's spine. Kruge opened his mouth, but before he could speak, his eyes rolled back. Dickens was only just able to grab the lamp, and with his other arm slow Kruge's fall, before Kruge collapsed at the foot of the gravestone.

Chapter Nineteen

Dickens struggled to get the taller Kruge on his feet and inside the sanctuary to the pew where they were before. Kruge sobbed mournfully, "I am done, Mr. Dickens. Condemned for eternity. Consigned to roast in the same flames that lick the man I loathed in life, and who will haunt me in death."

"Eben," Dickens addressed Kruge by his given name for the first time, "what happened out there?"

Kruge's eyes rolled in their sockets. "Where is the forgiveness, Mr. Dickens? Where is the mercy I have sought with all that is within me? Where is this God of yours? Have I not recanted? Have I not made amends as quickly as the world allows?" Kruge cried out again in abject agony, "Admit it, Mr. Dickens. Admit the lie! There is no forgiveness. Not for the unforgiveable. A man's deeds convict him when they are such as mine!"

Kruge buried his face in his hands.

Dickens knelt before the whimpering Kruge. "Eben, tell me what happened in the cemetery. What did you see?"

Kruge raised his head, a dazed look on his face. "But you were there . . ."

"Eben, the only people in the cemetery were you and I. I swear it. There was no one else in the cemetery."

"Surely you saw him . . . heard him . . . ! And what of the writing on the stone?"

Dickens shook his head. "I swear I did not. There was no one, no sound but the wind and thunder, and no change in your stone, Eben."

"You lie, Mr. Dickens," Kruge snapped angrily. "Why do you taunt me?"

"It serves me no purpose to lie, Eben," Dickens replied as gently as he could. "We were alone, and the only voice I heard was yours."

Kruge's anger gave way to bewilderment. "But he was there, Mr. Dickens. I swear it. As real as I am to you."

"Your . . . angel?"

"Yes, Yes! Gabriel, my angel! He was there . . . in white . . . as before." Kruge's eyes widened with fear. "Or do you suppose he is a demon?"

"What did he say to you, Eben?"

Kruge groaned in resignation, "That he cannot change what is on the stone."

"Your gravestone?"

"Of course, my stone," Kruge exclaimed, irritation in his voice.

"But there was . . . is nothing on the stone, Eben. Nothing. It is the same as before . . . a smooth face of granite, except for your name."

"No! There *was* writing," Kruge protested vehemently. "I saw it. I felt it. I always see it . . . though only for a time . . . minutes, and then it is gone."

"The stone is blank, Eben. It was never otherwise," Dickens spoke bluntly and slowly, as if doing so might make his words more convincing. "Why would there be writing on the stone, Eben? You are alive!"

"I am not mad," Kruge wailed, pounding his head with his fists. "I am not crazy!"

"And I am not lying, sir," Dickens replied, almost in a whisper.

For a long moment, neither said anything.

"All right, then . . ." Dickens picked his words carefully, "the writing on the stone, what did it say?"

"As before . . . my name; my date of birth, *February 25, 1783*. And, at the bottom, the same words . . . the words that burn my soul . . ."

"Yes," Dickens pressed, "What words, Eben?"

Kruge shrieked in anguish, "*HELL IS THINE HOME*"!

The bizarre pronouncement unnerved Dickens, despite his conviction that Kruge was hallucinating.

Kruge stood up and straightened himself. He stared blankly at Dickens and then at the door to the cemetery. He took a deep breath, as though a man condemned to the gallows, steeled to go bravely. "When I am in the cemetery, which is nearly every night since beginning my restitutions, the writing is the same, each night, and I hope against hope that the next night it might be different. But it isn't. I was here last night, Mr. Dickens. When you were asleep at the hotel, I was here, and there was no change."

"Yet upon my soul, Eben, there was no one else in the cemetery. There was nothing upon the stone but your name."

"That you did not see it, Mr. Dickens," Kruge replied in despondent tones, "that you cannot see what haunts me, or hear or touch its message, diminishes not one tittle its reality for me. My ears, my eyes, my hands bear witness . . . that I am the most wretched of men . . ." Kruge raised his eyes to the cross. "God, if you exist, have mercy on me, strike me down . . . make an end of it. What more can I do? I have righted so many wrongs my wealth is nearly gone . . . yet, I've no credit for it. I am done."

"Eben," Dickens said, after Kruge had been silent for a long minute, "I am a writer, not a priest, not a preacher. But I know human nature. I believe I know it in every form, and I know this, that doing good is always to your credit, but in and of itself, doing good things does not bring peace with God. For myself, I write and speak for the poor, neglected, orphaned, and widowed, and give to charities I can't number, but none of it gains me favor with God. What I do, no matter my motives, does not merit me restitution with God. Why? Because God is perfect and holy, and I am not . . . none of us are."

"Then of all men, I am to be pitied!" Kruge cried out.

"Not true, my friend." Dickens laid his hand gently on Kruge's shoulder. "What you experience each night, I cannot know, and, in truth, I wish not to know. But what you see on that stone, whether or not you are the only one who sees it, I believe it can change."

"But how, if not yet?"

"That will be God's doing, not yours."

"But you know my sin, sir."

"All of us fail, Eben . . . it is our human nature. And try as I might, I cannot maintain the high road. Eventually, I fail . . . fall prey to pride, arrogance, or some other temptation, and am again on my knees. But God is faithful to forgive, Eben. And that is what Christmas is all about, God doing for us what we cannot do for ourselves. Indeed, the only difference between your uncle and me is Christmas." Dickens paused. "In your Gabriel, I perceive God reaching out to you. Your Gabriel is a blessing, and whether angel or ghost does not matter. God, who knows your past, present, and future, is reaching out to you through him."

Kruge stared long at Dickens. "What more can I do to, sir?"

"Eben, do you believe in God?"

The bluntness of Dickens's question was like a blow to Kruge. Tears welled up in his eyes.

"Eben," Dickens pressed, "do you believe God exists?"

"I . . . I want to . . . with all my heart . . . I want to . . ." Kruge stammered. "But . . . I . . . don't know. I don't know if it is in me to believe."

The honesty of Kruge's words stung Dickens.

"Then you must persevere, Eben. For it is God's promise, that if you seek him with all your heart, you will find him. And, my friend, you must know this; that in my life I have struggled more than once with faith, for me the trappings of religion, the legalism preached by so many, confusing my understanding of who God is and what he wants of me. But I always come back, because I know he is real, that he loves me, that heaven is real. And so, Eben, can you do that? Can you persevere?"

Chapter Twenty

After Kruge had sufficiently recovered, Dickens accompanied him to his house, the two of them walking side-by-side in silence. Nearing the large house, in which there was a single candle burning in a downstairs' window, it was Kruge who broke the silence. "Mr. Dickens, you are a good man, and our time together has been short . . . but I must beg a favor of you."

"Then do so," Dickens replied. "If it is in my power, I shall be pleased to grant it."

When Kruge had made known his request, Dickens halted abruptly. "You would ask that of me?"

"You may deny me, of course, and I would be no way the wiser once you are back in England, but that is my request."

At the front door to Kruge's house, Dickens parted from Kruge with only a handshake and a nod, and made his way to the wheelwright's shop, where he found the key left by Micawley. He lay down exhausted on the pallet provided, and fell soon fast asleep.

The next morning, having slept briefly, but as a stone, Dickens awoke to early morning light streaming through the east window. He splashed his face with water from a washbowl provided by Micawley and wiped his face with a hand towel. He sensed the unfamiliar stubble of an infant beard. Quickly dressed, he sat at Micawley's desk and penned a note of thanks to the wheelwright and his son. A barefoot youth at the livery greeted him, and promptly hitched Colonel to the buggy, and by eight o'clock the town of Cornwall lay behind Dickens.

Dickens arrived at the West Point hotel famished, and over a plate of fried eggs, diced potatoes, thick bacon, toasted bread, butter, and jam, and coffee related to Catherine and Captain Roe that his trip, while enjoyable enough, did not produce as he had hoped, that Mr. Eben Kruge, while indeed a quirky man, was not the stuff of his stories, but that he had found in the whole of his absence the peace he had been missing for several months.

Before he and Catherine boarded the one o'clock steamer, Dickens made a point, to Roe's great delight, of endorsing all of the purloined books in the hotel proprietor's collection, and after doing so relaying a decision that had been made, not by him, but by others, the meat of which gave Roe great reason to celebrate. The Pickwick Club in special session, the venerable Samuel Pickwick presiding, and with Snodgrass, Winkle, and Tupman in concurrence, and by unanimous vote, which of course was required for any club measure to carry, determined that Captain Roe was henceforth to consider himself a full member of the Pickwick Club, with all the rights and privileges attendant thereto, and could expect a formal certificate to that end, along with his swatch, the coveted PC emblem embossed thereon, in post forthwith.

As the packet steamed around the bend of the river, heading south and approaching the village of Garrison perched on the east side of the Hudson, Dickens, Catherine beside him, stood aft of the boat with borrowed eyeglass hoping to see the spire of the Cornwall Presbyterian Church. But Butter Hill hid the entire town from view. Regardless, he offered a silent prayer for all the souls he had encountered in that town, his last thought being of the man, Eben Kruge.

Spending the night in New York City, on the following day, Dickens and Catherine boarded a sailing packet, a spacious three-masted square-rigger, and, under a blue sky and freshing breeze, headed home, observing on the last day of June the skyline of Liverpool.

Epilogue

Immediately upon returning to England, there was a tear-filled reunion of the Dickens family, and for the next two days Dickens did anything and everything with his beloved children, assigning each a new pet name and conjuring up new stories to delight them. Thereafter, with irrepressible energy, he invested himself in completing his accounting of the new country, America, and adding to its end a section on the crown colony Canada. To that purpose, he used his journal and borrowed letters that he had sent home to Forster, Macready and others. Chapman and Hall published the travel log, *American Notes*, in October of 1842, the reception of which was a disappointment to Dickens. The book received a cold reaction by the American press and its general public, which were expecting an altogether different report from one they had so admired and embraced. It was of small consolation to Dickens that most of his American literary friends, including Irving, thought it entirely accurate. Several pointed out that their country, unlike England, being in its infancy, was thin-skinned and ill suited to critical review.

Still the book was read extensively in the new country, if only to vilify its author, but read as before, in pirated versions, in print and circulation even before his new friend, Longfellow, returned home from a tour of Europe with freshly printed copies given him by Dickens himself. In England, however, where the book received generally high reviews, sales proved less than inspiring, Forster suggesting that perhaps the wounds of having been out done by a colony had not yet fully healed.

Consequently, Dickens immersed his mind in his next serial work, which, after agonizing over its principal's name, he titled *Martin Chuzzlewit*, a story set in England and an examination of selfishness. In his mind, it was his finest work. Hall and Chapman circulated its first monthly edition in January of 1843, but its sales were less than half of what had been forecast, and remained so in the months that followed.

Dickens was beside himself with self-doubt, self-examination, and a haunting fear of life repeating itself. The costs of renovations to the home on Devonshire Terrace were more than double what he had expected. In April, Catherine announced yet another visit by the stork, and in late summer, after Dickens had decided that his serial characters should take a trip to America, which only marginally improved sales, he was led to understand that Chapman and Hall was about to dock his monthly payments for *Martin Chuzzlewit* by twenty-five percent, something they pointed out was their right under contract.

Hence, it was of no little effect that in October of 1843, alone in his study, Catherine and the children already bedded, he opened a letter that he had received only that day. It was posted from America.

Eben Kruge, Esquire
Cornwall, New York

September 18, 1843

To my friend and confident, Charles Dickens,

First, let me say that I know you better, having just now finished the last of your books. Your heart, sir, is indeed for the downtrodden, as is the one you follow, who is now the one I follow. Upon your departure, I took up the good book once again, and read the balance of its second part, and then from the beginning both parts. What a patient and merciful God we have, my friend, wanting only that we would love one another as we do ourselves, something I've always had a problem with, given I loved myself not at all. But that, too, has changed, as I may not be such a bad sort after all.

None will know what I relate to you in this letter. But if anyone should know it, it should be you.

When you visited me two Junes ago, it was not in my nature to share with you things that I will tell you now, as I prepare to travel. The afternoon when I left you until rejoining you at the George Washington Inn, I visited and was attended to by my doctor, a Charles Worthy, in Newburgh. Having treated me for some time, he confirmed to me what he had earlier thought, that I had a cancer and but months to live, not more than a year. The man who approached us in the restaurant was his assistant, bearing written instructions Worthy had forgotten to give me on the regimen I should follow.

It was in that light, you saw me that night at the cemetery, during which, I apologize for my actions. Fear does that, and the actions of a man with no hope must be a sight to see.

Anyway, upon finishing the good book and after attending services weekly with a dear friend, whom you know, at the church where you and I were, me favoring the pew you and I sat on, I am pleased to announce and profess before our mutual God, that one midnight, my angel, old Gabriel, bid me again to look at the stone, which I did.

My friend, IT WAS CHANGED—as I felt in my heart it must soon be. Upon the stone were the words, *Rest in Peace with Almighty God*. But that was some months ago, and I must tell you that I am now a sight only for the strong, and shall not see another Christmas.

And there it is. My tears rain on this letter, my joy so great.

I leave on my journey having righted every wrong that I can remember, and others likely not my own, but so much the better, as I'll take nothing with me. Perhaps when I arrive, there will be a father and mother to greet me. And, yes, I have forgiven my uncle, and that, I think, was what changed me and the stone.

Mr. Dickens, though I will gleefully await your arrival, I'm not suggesting you hurry, and I now release you from your promise and grant you full permission to tell your story in any fashion you see fit.

What a glorious day to . . .

Here, the writing ceased, save for a shaky line of ink down the sheet of vellum. On a separate sheet of vellum was a note from Micawley.

Dear Mr. Dickens,

Eben went to his maker at his desk and with quill pen in hand, and so I suppose he was wrong, as I too know the contents of his letter, though not fully its meaning, which I suppose is well enough. I say to you with the greatest conviction that it was divine fate that brought you to Cornwall and to us. A day after your departure, Eben comes to my store wanting a word, and in the space of an afternoon the chasm of enmity between us, fixed I thought for eternity, was gone. He declared that I now owned my shop free and clear, and that within the week I would receive the cancelled mortgage, which I did. In that same meeting, he told me that Daniel had come to his office that morning, and that he had made amends with him, too, and had given him ownership of the house legally stolen from his mother—with one stipulation—that he be allowed to remain, as a lodger, along with his house keeper, and that he would pay handsomely for the right to be a lodger. We three are on the instant the best of chums, as in days past, young schoolboys, now grown old, but not so different, and I suppose I am the friend he mentions in his letter.

Sir, I will tell you that Eben lived strong and well the next year and more, enjoying Christmas more fully than a dozen of the most faithful, and he died without a penny, having dispersed all, including a handsome sum to the church. Only in his last days did his energy and appearance suffer. And it goes to his credit that his funeral was better attended than any I can recall in Cornwall.

I was pleased in reading your *American Notes* to see no mention of your coming to see us, and I understand, and that is best. How could such a thing be explained? And so, in closing, I wish you and yours God's rich blessings.

Your humble servant, and with great affection,

Jedidiah Micawley

Postscript: Young James sends his best, and this year his class is reading Oliver Twist.

After reading Kruge's letter and Micawley's note a second time, and after wiping his eyes repeatedly, Dickens rose from his desk, walked the few steps to the firebox, and inserted the letter and note. As they burned, he resolved that none, not even Forster, would know of Eben Kruge, vowing it was the least he could do for the man he would never forget. Drying his eyes, he returned to his desk, drew a fresh stack of vellum from the drawer, cut a fresh quill, dipped the inkwell, and put pen to paper to write what had been on his mind the entire trip home to England. When quill scratched vellum, and ink appeared, his soul tingled over what danced in his head, a story that would span one day and feature not one, but three ghosts conveying the whole of life—past, present, and future—and which might uniquely stir hearts and tongues to properly and for many years to come honor the season and meaning of Christmas.

Acknowledgements

First, I want to give all glory to the source of Christmas and his amazing grace, without whom there would be no *Carol*, no *Kruge*, or any other such work. Next, I want to acknowledge Charles Dickens for being who he was and doing what he did; my incredible family, from oldest to youngest, who have filled my life with joy unending; my circle of friends, inestimable in number and ever increasing; and my older brother, Jim, now in heaven, who first heard my ramblings about *Eben Kruge* and encouraged me to write the story.

Rich Adams

Author's Notes

Eben Kruge, while fictional, connects many factual dots about the man, Charles Dickens, his background, and the circumstances leading up to his frenzied writing of the most famous of all Christmas fables. Following the failed attempt by Dickens to witness the worship service by the Shakers at their settlement near Lebanon, New York, he, his wife Catherine, and Catherine's maid, Anne Brown (not featured in the story), arrived at West Point on June 4, 1842, and departed June 6. Spending one night in New York City, they then depart for England. Dickens had a close relationship with Washington Irving, and did visit his Sunnyside home in Tarrytown, New York. And, indeed, there was a matriarchal tribe of Lenni Lenape Indians living in the environs of Schunemunk Mountain before their deportation to distant reservations. Interestingly, Dickens had a somewhat conflicted encounter with Edgar Allen Poe before his return to England.

After returning to England, Dickens's first publication was his American travelogue, *American Notes*, published October 18, 1842. In January 1843, he began writing monthly installments of his next serial work, *Martin Chuzzlewit*, which would not be completed until July 1844. Beginning in October 1843 and over only a six-week period, Dickens completed his first fictional work since returning to England, *A Christmas Carol*, a phenomenal achievement, even for Dickens, given he was also writing monthly installments of *Martin Chuzzlewit*.

At the time of this story, Charles Dickens is thirty years old. His gifts have been recognized—he is a world-renowned writer and orator, a beloved husband, father, son, brother, friend, a benefactor of the downtrodden, and, by trial and error, becoming a better businessman. He enjoys hard work and, even more, a good time with friends. And, most assuredly, he is still hiding from the world the shame of his youth; the time his family was in the Marshalsea, a debtors' prison in London, and, himself, a common laborer in a boot-blacking factory. And not until after his death, would such be made known to the world by his first biographer, dear friend, and executor, John Forster.

Prior to writing *A Christmas Carol*, Dickens's only relevant visit to the supernatural appears to have been a somewhat comedic segment of *The Pickwick Papers*, in which old Wardle tells of Gabriel Grubb, a curmudgeon church sexton, who knocks the head of a boy singing a Christmas carol, and for it, is visited by goblins.

Dickens was a doting parent, who fathered the four children named in the story and eventually six more, and at the time of the story was very much in love with Catherine. His later life is well chronicled by various biographers who have recorded his humanness, though; it is unlikely that Dickens, himself, ever had any supposition that he was other than imperfect.

But what is perhaps not so well known about Dickens is that he was a deeply spiritual man. An opponent of religious legalism and for a time a Unitarian, he returned to the Anglican Church. He was in the habit of praying twice daily, morning and evening, and he continually read his Bible. In 1849, he concluded the writing of his own New Testament account of the life and teachings of Jesus Christ, entitled *The Life of Our Lord*, drawn from the Gospel of Luke, and written expressly for his children and not for publication, and which he read aloud to his children every Christmas. This little book, which has since been published (1934), begins:

> "My Dear Children, I am very anxious that you should know something about the History of Jesus Christ. For everybody ought to know about Him. No one ever lived who was so good, so kind, so gentle, and so sorry for all people who did wrong, or were in any way ill or miserable, as He was."

And in Dickens's last will and testament, executed upon his death at age fifty-nine, Dickens states:

> "I commit my soul to the mercy of God through our Lord and Savior Jesus Christ, and I exhort my dear children humbly to try to guide themselves by the teaching of the New Testament in its broad spirit, and to put no faith in any man's narrow construction of its letter here and there."

About The Author

Rich Adams and his wife have two married children, several grandchildren, reside part of the year in Sandestin, Florida, part of the year in Denver, Colorado, and are members of the Destin United Methodist Church.

After graduating from West Point (Class of 1967) and seven years of active military duty, including service in Vietnam, he and his family settled in Austin, Texas, where he began a career as a consulting engineer. He later moved the family to Baton Rouge, Louisiana, where he founded and sixteen years later sold an engineering and environmental services company. He is active in West Point alumni affairs and the many activities of his class, and has served as an adjunct assistant professor at the Academy, as well as an adjunct professor to the School of Engineering and Applied Science at Southern Methodist University.

Adams' first novel, *The Parting: A Story of West Point on the Eve of the Civil War (www.RichardBarlowAdams.com)*, is a true story of the West Point Class of 1861, and draws upon, among other things, his background as the first of three brothers to graduate from West Point, sons of an Army colonel. *The Parting* is the recipient of a five-star Clarion Foreword Book Review.

As he pursues his writing, Adams continues to serve as a consulting forensic engineer, and is a part-time ski instructor at Beaver Creek, Colorado. He also enjoys sharing his faith, traveling, lecturing, golfing, hiking, and biking.

Green Apple Photography (www.greenapplephotos.com)

CPSIA information can be obtained at www.ICGtesting.com
Printed in the USA
LVOW100424141112

307231LV00002B/5/P

9 781479 742318